For Connie

First published 2015 by Macmillan Children's Books
an imprint of Pan Macmillan
20 New Wharf Road, London N1 9RR
Associated companies throughout the world
www.panmacmillan.com

ISBN 978-1-4472-7789-7

1 3 5 7 9 8 6 4 2

A CIP catalogue record for this book is available from the British Library.

Printed and bound in China

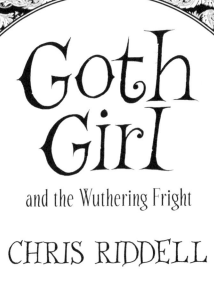

Goth Girl

and the Wuthering Fright

CHRIS RIDDELL

MACMILLAN
CHILDREN'S BOOKS

THIS BOOK CONTAINS COGWHEEL
FOOT NOTES WRITTEN BY A
CALCULATING MACHINE INVENTED
BY CHARLES CABBAGE

Chapter One

Sitting in one of the wing-back chairs in the library of Ghastly-Gorm Hall, Ada Goth was reading her father's latest book. She smiled to herself as she turned the page. Leather-bound volumes lined the carved mahogany bookcases that were built into the walls of the library, and each bookcase had a ladder on brass wheels, for reaching the higher shelves. Busts of Roman emperors with interesting haircuts looked down from the very top, the firelight glinting on their curls and ringlets. Not that Ada noticed. She was engrossed.

Ada was the only child of Lord Goth, England's foremost cycling poet. He was away in London, giving a talk and having his hair styled at the literary hair salon of Scribble and Quiff's, but he would be back for Christmas.

GHASTLY-GORM
HALL

THE EVEN-MORE-
SECRET GARDEN

THE
SECRET GARDEN

THE BACK OF
BEYOND GARDEN
(UNFINISHED)

THE OLD
ICE HOUSE

THE BROKEN
WING

THE
UNSTABLE
STABLES

THE
HOBBY-HORSE
STABLES

THE
ALPINE
GNOME
ROCKERY

THE
VENETIAN
TERRACE

'THE WEST

N
E
S

THE AVENUE OF OUTRAGEOUS FORTUNE

THE
SLOUGH
OF
DESPOND

METAPHORICAL
SMITH'S HOBBY-HORSE
RACECOURSE

THE GRAVEL PATH OF CONCEIT

THE POND
OF
INTROSPECTION

ADA'S NICKNAMES FOR THE BUSTS...

TESTY TRAJAN | DOPEY DOMITIAN | VESPASIAN NO-NOSE | JULIUS SNEEZER | HAIRY HADRIAN | BIG-EAR AUGUST

Christmas at Ghastly-Gorm Hall was usually a quiet affair. The bells of the little church of Gormless St Hilda's were rung and the local shepherds gathered for the ancient ceremony of the washing of the socks while the inhabitants of the little hamlet of Gormless exchanged gifts of stockings containing small oranges and lumps of coal.

Ada wanted to finish her father's book before he returned. It was a very exciting story written in verse, called *The Pilgrimage of Harolde the Kid*, about the travels of a young goat. Ada had just got to the part where Harolde climbs the Alps to nibble

4

THE
PILGRIMAGE
OF
HAROLDE
THE
KID

mountain moss when she heard the squeak of little brass wheels. Looking up from the book, Ada saw a ladder moving past Hairy Hadrian and towards Big-Eared Augustus.

A small monkey in an even smaller hat was gliding past the bookshelves, holding on to the ladder with one hand and pulling himself along with the other. As Ada watched, the monkey brought the ladder to a halt and carefully selected a book from the top-most shelf. It then pushed the ladder on to the end of the bookcase, scampered down the rungs and hurried out of the door.

How curious, thought Ada. She was about to return to *The Pilgrimage of Harolde the Kid* when she caught sight of a movement out of the corner of her eye. Ada peered around the wing of her wing-back chair. A second monkey was pushing a second ladder along the bookcase just behind her. Ada watched as the monkey, who had a three-volume survey of Ireland under his arm, came to a stop and carefully replaced the heavy books on the shelf, one after the other, before sliding down the ladder and skipping out of the library. Curiouser and curiouser, thought Ada, and returned to her book. There was an illustration of Harolde having a conversation with a wild-looking mountain goat with curly horns. She smiled – this was just the sort of book she liked. After all, thought Ada, what's the use of a book without pictures or conversations? It was what one of her governesses had told her. Ada couldn't remember which one.*

Ada had been taught by seven governesses . . .

COGWHEEL
FOOT NOTE
. . . .

*In fact Jane Ear, Ada's third governess, had overheard a former pupil called Charlie Dodgson saying this as he drew a comic strip in the margin of his mathematics book, and liked to repeat it as if it was her own idea.

LUCY BORGIA WAS ADA'S CURRENT GOVERNESS AND WAS ON A MOONLIT TOUR OF WHITBY WITH LORD SYDNEY WHIMSY.

MORAG MACBEE WAS NOW HEADMISTRESS OF THE EDINBURGH ACADEMY FOR YOUNG LADIES OF QUALITY.

HEBE POPPINS WAS MARRIED TO A CHIMNEY SWEEP AND HAD A DAUGHTER CALLED MARY.

JANE EAR WAS RUNNING A SMALL SCHOOL IN YORKSHIRE.

NANNY DARLING WAS GUARDING THE CRÈCHE AT THE KENSINGTON GARDENS NURSERY.

BECKY BLUNT WAS THE SPORTS MISTRESS AT ROTTENDEAN SCHOOL IN THE FASHIONABLE SEASIDE RESORT OF BRIGHTON.

MARIANNE DELACROIX HAD A TALENTED SON CALLED EUGENE.

Ada turned the page and continued reading.

From lofty crag oft tipped with misty fog,

To lowland vale steeped deep in bog,

Harolde his vertiginous pilgrimage did make,

Stopping only for tea and cake.

'Baa!' quoth he, and 'Bleat!' he blew,

For these were the only words he knew . . .

Just then, a third monkey walked past Ada's chair clutching a book almost as large as itself. 'Catalogue of Public Nuisances' it said in gold letters on the spine, 'by Charles Cabbage'. When Ada caught the monkey's eye, it stopped and looked a little awkward. Then it reached into the waistcoat it was wearing and took out a tiny tin cup which it held out towards Ada with a little shake. 'I'm terribly sorry,' said Ada politely, 'but I don't have anything to give you.'

The monkey shrugged, put the cup away and tipped its little hat before walking on, balancing the book rather elegantly on its head.

It reached the door and slipped out. 'And curiouser!' exclaimed Ada, putting down her book. She walked across the library and was about to follow the monkey out of the door when she glanced through one of the tall windows. Ada gasped.

Outside, the wintry sky was a deep, dark grey and snow

was falling. Large snowflakes danced and swirled as they fluttered down to land, covering the house and grounds of Ghastly-Gorm Hall in a carpet of white. In the distance, the elegant outline of the Sensible Folly was being softened and blurred while the surface of the lake of extremely coy carp was stiff with ice. The dear-deer park was completely covered and the Venetian terrace and Overly Ornamental Fountain had all but disappeared. Ada pressed her nose up to the glass of the window and watched winter descend on her home. It was a magical sight and she would have watched the snow falling for the rest of the afternoon if one of the monkeys had not returned a few minutes later. When it saw her the monkey politely lifted its hat. Then it climbed a ladder, selected a book on writing secret codes and left the library. This time Ada followed. The monkey made its way through several drawing rooms . . .

Ada picked up a periodical that the monkey had
accidentally knocked off one of the coffee tables.

HAIR & HOUNDS

JOURNAL OF LITERARY HAIR SALONS AND SPORTING LIFE

Winter Issue

ANNOUNCEMENTS

RUGBY SCHOOL ANNOUNCES THE NEW SPORT OF

'MUDDY FIELD WRESTLING'

DETAILS PAGE xxxiii

SCRIBBLE AND QUIFF

TO EMPLOY HAIR-COMBING CATS AT THEIR MONTHLY POETRY READINGS

DETAILS PAGE xxi

LORD GOTH TO HOST THE GHASTLY-GORM

LITERARY DOG SHOW

ENTRANTS BY INVITATION ONLY – DETAILS PAGE xii

DISTINGUISHED NOVELIST MR CHRISTOPHER PRIESTLEY ESQ. SPORTING A CAMBRIDGE QUIFF WITH HIS FENLAND SCHNAUZER 'UNCLE MONTAGUE'

DETAILS PAGE viii

IN THIS ISSUE –
HOUSE TRAINING & QUILL SHARPENING

'So you've seen the announcement, young mistress,' said a wheezing voice as dry and dusty as chalk. Ada looked round to see Maltravers standing in the other doorway. Beside him two large poodles, one white and one black, strained at the end of their leashes.

'Your father got the idea for the literary dog show when I told him how well Belle and Sebastian were getting on with their training . . .' The indoor gamekeeper (who was also the outdoor butler) smiled, his long grey face creasing into a thousand wrinkles and his lips spreading to reveal a jumble of tombstone teeth the colour of tea. He patted the luxuriant pompom on each poodle's head. Ada didn't like Maltravers very much. With his habit of creeping silently through the house listening at doors and peering through keyholes, he made Ada shudder whenever they met. But ever since Lord Goth had given him the poodles, Maltravers had been a changed man. He still looked strange, but now he smiled a lot and even whistled little tunes when he took the poodles for their indoor walks.

Ada looked at the announcements column on the cover of the periodical.

'A dog show?' she said.

'Exciting, isn't it, young mistress?' Maltravers

wheezed happily. He tugged the poodles' leashes. 'Come on, my darlings! Lots of work to do.'

The indoor gamekeeper and outdoor butler set off towards the Whine Cellars beneath Ghastly-Gorm Hall, where the poodles had their kennel.

Ada went over to the door the monkey had run through and knocked on it. It was the door to the Chinese drawing room.

'Come in,' said a harassed-sounding voice.

Chapter Two

Charles Cabbage was sitting at a large desk in the middle of the Chinese drawing room. The desk was piled high with books from the library and the floor was littered with sheets of paper covered in calculations written in green ink. At the far end of the room, taking up the entire wall, was a complicated-looking machine with cogs and gear wheels and cranking handles. This was the calculating machine that Charles Cabbage was making for Lord Goth. He called it the Cogwheel Brain and he'd been working on it for such a long time that Ada suspected her father had forgotten all about the machine and its inventor. Ghastly-Gorm Hall was an extremely large house, and visitors were always turning up with invitations of one sort or another, or to paint the ceilings, landscape the

gardens or install the latest household appliances. Usually these visitors stayed for a few days or a week or two at the most.

But Charles Cabbage was taking far longer than that to build his calculating machine. Not that Ada minded, because the longer he took, the more time Ada could spend with Emily, his daughter, who was Ada's best friend and an extremely accomplished watercolourist. Emily and her brother William were away at school, but they came to stay at Ghastly-Gorm Hall in the holidays.

'Why, Miss Goth, how nice to see you,' said Dr Cabbage, without looking up from the sheet of paper he was writing on. He moved to the other side of the desk and Ada saw that he was sitting on a chair whose wheels were powered by clockwork. Dr Cabbage came to a stop and picked up a book from the top of a precarious pile.

'Do you know how many

broken factory windows there are in Manchester?'
he asked, turning the pages.

'I don't think I do,' said Ada.

'Too many!' said Dr Cabbage, shutting the
book and trundling back around the desk,
knocking sheets of paper to the floor as he did so.

'As for small boys rolling hoops through the streets,' he muttered, 'it's a public nuisance of the worst kind.'

'It is?' said Ada, looking for any sign of monkeys. Apart from the desk and the half-built calculating machine, the Chinese drawing room had been cleared of its furniture. The forbidden footstools, willow-pattern divans and great stall of China – a sideboard for displaying crockery – had all been moved to the broken wing for storage. The broken wing at the back of Ghastly-Gorm Hall was Ada's favourite part of the house. Its rooms were full of interesting things that had been put there and then forgotten about.

'Hoop-rolling in public should be stopped,' said Dr Cabbage, getting off his chair and rummaging beneath the desk. 'I propose a perfectly simple solution . . .' He emerged with a metal hoop in his hands, then slipped it over his head and began to do a strange gyrating dance, spinning the hoop around and around his ample waist.

'Instead of rolling one's hoop down the street, getting in people's way, a small boy can have hours of fun standing in one spot spinning it around his middle!'

'It does look fun,' said Ada.

'I've named it the hooligan hoop after some unruly children I met while inspecting empty factories – they could have benefited from this exercise,' said Dr Cabbage sternly, 'instead of breaking windows!'* Just then three monkeys popped their heads up from beneath the desk and began clapping excitedly.

'There you are!' exclaimed Ada.

Dr Cabbage let the hoop drop to the floor and stepped out of it. He sat down on the clockwork chair and jotted down a quick note.

The monkeys surrounded Ada, waving tiny tin cups at her.

'William! Heath!' said Dr Cabbage firmly, still without looking up, 'and you, Robinson! Put those cups away!'

The monkeys did as they were told.

'Now fetch the first three books on the eighth shelf of the ninth bookcase!'

COGWHEEL
FOOT NOTE
....
*Noel and Liam promised not to break any more factory windows and learned to play musical instruments instead.

THE COGWHEEL
BRAIN

William, Heath and Robinson skipped out of the Chinese drawing room.

'What are the books about?' asked Ada, impressed by how well trained the monkeys were.

'I've absolutely no idea,' said Dr Cabbage, gliding around his desk, searching for a fresh sheet of paper, 'but they're sure to be fascinating. They always are, and my library monkeys do enjoy fetching and returning them. It's a much more useful job than their last one.'

'What did they used to do?' Ada asked.

'They were organ-grinders' monkeys,' said Dr Cabbage with a shudder. 'The music of organ grinders in the streets is the worst public nuisance of them all!' he declared. 'My friends and I in the Extractors Club are dedicated to disrupting organ-grinders' music by persuading their monkeys to seek more useful employment.'

'How do you persuade them?' asked Ada doubtfully.

'Bananas help,' said Dr Cabbage. 'The

Extractors Club sent William, Heath and Robinson up from London yesterday and they seem to be adjusting well to life in the country. There's only one problem.'

He shut the book he'd begun reading, adjusted his spectacles and looked at Ada for the first time.

'I don't know whether you've noticed, Miss Goth –' he nodded towards the shuttered windows of the Chinese drawing room – 'but the weather has turned awfully cold and the monkeys don't have any winter clothes.'

'I'll see what I can do,' said Ada.

'I almost forgot, Miss Goth,' he added as Ada turned to leave the room. 'My daughter sent you a letter – so good to see my ideas for a postal system are catching on.'

Dr Cabbage handed Ada a letter with a green stamp on it before returning to the desk, which now looked even untidier.

A PENNY CABBAGE

Ada opened the letter . . .

The Windy Moor
School,
West Wuthering,
Yorkshire,
ENGLAND

Dearest Ada, School is fun and I've
made some new friends! After watercolour class,
my favourite lesson is poetry-and-walking,
which we do on the Moors. It is Very
Windy and the sonnet-bonnet you gave me
has been very useful.
        Looking forward to the holidays - I'll be
home by teatime on Tuesday!
            your dearest friend,
                Emily x

P.S. This letter has a green postage stamp
with the Prince Regent's portrait on it;
it is called a penny cabbage!

Chapter Three

Ada climbed the grand staircase past the portraits of the previous Lord Goths. She was thinking about Emily's letter, which had made her a bit sad. She would have loved to go to school with her best friend, but that would have meant her governess, Lucy Borgia, leaving Ghastly-Gorm Hall and Ada didn't want that.

Reaching the first-floor landing, Ada looked around to see if there were any early-evening ghosts about. Being so old and so big, Ghastly-Gorm Hall was home to quite a few ghosts who were all careful to appear at different times. The Beige Curate liked to slide down the banisters of the grand staircase around about teatime, while the Thinly Veiled Lady wandered the Venetian terrace sneezing softly at ten minutes to twelve on moonlit nights. Ada had found out about her in an

THE 1ST LORD GOTH, WHO SAT ON A VEGETABLE FROM THE NEW WORLD AND INVENTED MASHED POTATO.

THE 2nd LORD GOTH, THE CAVALIER CAVALIER, WHO WAS ALWAYS FORGETTING WHICH SIDE HE WAS ON IN THE CIVIL WAR.

THE 3RD LORD GOTH, WHO OWNED THE BALD IRISH WOLFHOUND CALLED PEEJAY.

THE 4TH LORD GOTH, WHO ROWED BONNET-PRINTS CHARLIE, A HIGHLAND HATMAKER, OVER THE SEA TO SKYE.

THE 5TH LORD GOTH, GRUMPY GRANDPAPA, WHO DISAPPROVED OF POETRY.

THE 6TH LORD GOTH, ADA'S FATHER, WHO IS WEARING ALBANIAN NATIONAL DRESS.

old book in the library.* It was almost six o'clock, which was when the two Annes generally played ghostly Tudor cricket on the first-floor landing, but this evening there was

COGWHEEL FOOT NOTE
....

*Ethelberta Enormousfeet was an Anglo-Saxon fell-walking princess who caught a fatal chill while wading in the water meadow that once existed on the site of the Venetian terrace. Ada had read all about her in *The Chronicles of the Vulnerable Bede*, a tear-stained history of England.

ANNE BOWL-IN

no sign of them. Ada made her way down the long gallery and along the corridor to her room.

Ada's bedroom was enormous, with an eight-poster bed on one side and a magnificent

ANNE OF PEEVES

fireplace on the other. Unfortunately it was a bit of a mess. Shoes, dresses, bonnets and hatboxes lay around on the Anatolian carpet, together with unfurled umbrellas, opened parasols and decorative fans. Ada tidied up, folding the dresses and putting the bonnets back in the hatboxes, lining the shoes up neatly in pairs and propping the umbrellas and parasols against the wall. She then took a pile of clothes through to her dressing room next door, where she found her new lady's maid lying on the Dalmatian divan.

Ada's previous lady's maid had been called Marylebone. She was a spectacled bear from Bolivia who had left Ghastly-Gorm Hall to get married. She now lived happily in a beautiful house in the Andes with her husband, General Simon Batholiver, and their newborn cub, Lucy. Marylebone

had been an excellent lady's maid, laying out Ada's clothes for her each day on the Dalmatian divan and keeping the bedroom and dressing room organized and tidy. The same could not be said of her replacement. But Ada didn't mind.

Fancyday Ambridge lived in the little hamlet of Gormless and sang in the Gormless Quire. Although she was forgetful and rather untidy, she was kind and cheerful and Ada had liked her from the moment they'd met. Fancyday was also musical and creative, and wore spectacles that reminded Ada of Marylebone. Each morning Fancyday would drive up to the Hall in her donkey and trap and spend the day looking through Ada's clothes and reading novels before driving home again.

'Why, Miss Ada!' Fancyday exclaimed. 'Is it six o'clock already? I quite lost track of the time on account of this book I'm reading.' She jumped up from the Dalmatian divan and raised the back of her hand to her forehead in a dramatical gesture.

'It is a truth universally acknowledged that

a talented singer in
possession of a good
voice must be in
want of a musical
production,'
Fancyday recited
from the first page
of her book, before
closing the book with
a flourish and
tossing it on to
the Dalmatian
divan.

'It's all about
Elizabeth Bonnett,
a simple country
girl with a
song in her
heart who
meets a
dashing

PROMPT AND PREJUDICE BY PLAIN AUSTEN

dancing master, Mr Darcy-Bussell.' Fancyday waltzed around the dressing room, using one of Ada's frocks as an imaginary partner. When she reached the door she gave a little gasp and dropped the frock on the floor.

'I almost forgot!' she exclaimed. 'Quire practice tonight! I'll see you tomorrow, Miss Ada!'

Fancyday danced out of the dressing room, across the bedroom and out of the door, narrowly avoiding Ruby the outer-pantry maid, who was coming in. Ruby was holding a tray with Ada's supper on it. She looked wide-eyed and anxious.

'If you don't mind, Ada,' she said, 'I'll put this down here by the fire and get back to the pantry before those ghostly ladies appear.'

'The two Tudor Annes?' said Ada. 'I heard they died after an argument over cricket. One hit the other over the head with a bat and then slipped on a ball and fell down the stairs. I'm not sure which was which, but I'll try to find out.'

'If you do, you can tell us at the next meeting of the Attic Club,' said Ruby hastily, putting the tray on the more-than-occasional table and hurrying from the room.

A moment later Ada heard a little scream and the sound of Ruby's footsteps clattering down the stairs as the two

Tudor Annes called, 'Howzat!' after her in ghostly voices.

The Attic Club met once a week in secret in the attics of Ghastly-Gorm Hall to share observations and discoveries. Emily and William Cabbage had founded the club and Ada and Ruby were members, along with Arthur Halford the hobby-horse groom and Kingsley the chimney caretaker. They wrote down their findings in *The Chimney Pot — Journal of the Attic Club*.

Ruby was very shy and the ghosts of Ghastly-Gorm Hall scared her, but she was brave in other ways, not least in working for Mrs Beat'em the cook, who shouted at her kitchen maids and often made them cry. Ada finished tidying up after her lady's maid and sat down in front of the fire for supper. Mrs Beat'em's roast beef and Ghastlyshire pudding was delicious and her burbleberry syllabub was perfect. Outside the snow was still falling and Ada hoped it wouldn't be too deep for Fancyday's donkey and trap.

This cold weather was a nuisance for some, thought Ada, but it made Ghastly-Gorm look rather beautiful and it was almost Christmas after all. She gave a little shiver of excitement. Tomorrow she would see Emily and hear all about school.

When Ada had eaten her supper she went into her dressing room and opened the wardrobe. She rummaged around inside and pulled out a bag of wool her French governess, Marianne Delacroix, had given her, and two knitting needles.

✳

THE ATTIC CLUB

ADA RESEARCHED
GHOSTLY SIGHTINGS
AND WROTE ABOUT
THEIR CAUSES.

EMILY CABBAGE
DREW PICTURES
OF PLANTS, FLOWERS
AND INTERESTING THINGS.

WILLIAM CABBAGE
COLLECTED DECORATIVE
PATTERNS AND
WALL PAPER.

RUBY KIPLING
WAS COOKERY
CORRESPONDENT OF
'THE CHIMNEY POT'.

ARTHUR HALFORD
WROTE ABOUT
HOBBY-HORSE
RACES.

KINGSLEY TRAVERS
CATALOGUED ORNAMENTAL
CHIMNEY AND FIREPLACE
DESIGNS.

That evening and most of the next day Ada sat
in her bedroom in front of the fire, knitting.
The only sounds were the crackle of the logs
on the fire and the clickety-click of the 'lefarge'
knitting needles. A small boy had arrived mid-
morning with a note from Fancyday telling
Ada that her donkey was refusing to leave his
stable so she wouldn't be coming to work today.
That was just as well, thought Ada,
because she was too busy to tidy up
after her. As the great-uncle clock
struck three, Ada put down the
knitting needles and set off for
the Chinese
drawing
room.

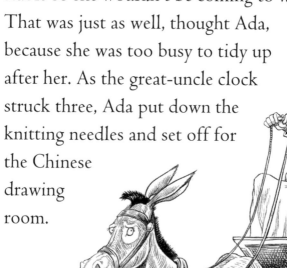

MADDENING CLAUDE
THE STUBBORN DONKEY

When she arrived, Ada found Dr Cabbage and the three library monkeys waiting for her. 'There you are, Miss Goth!' exclaimed Charles Cabbage. He was a little out of breath because he'd been spinning his hooligan hoop. William, Heath and Robinson each had small hoops of their own and were busy spinning them around their middles.

'It keeps them warm,' explained Dr Cabbage.

'I hope these will keep them even warmer,' said Ada, holding up the three suits she'd knitted. 'I also had time to make them some Gothkerchiefs just like my father's,' she added, handing out the clothes. The monkeys seemed delighted, even though, when they tried them on, the suits were a little too big. She helped them tie their Gothkerchiefs and stood back to admire the result . . .

'Excellent!' declared Dr Cabbage. 'You must wrap up warm yourself, Miss Goth.'

'I must?' said Ada.

'Yes.' Dr Cabbage smiled. 'If you want to come with us to meet the Ghastlyshire mail coach. Emily and William are coming home today and, what's more, we have to pick up the entrants of the literary dog show!'

Chapter Four

The five of them set off for the little hamlet of Gormless in Charles Cabbage's 'Difference Engine'. It was a steam-driven traction engine with a shovel-shaped seat and a steering wheel at the front and a tall funnel at the back. The Difference Engine was quite slow and noisy but had no difficulty ploughing through the snow as it trundled down the drive and out of the gates.

'Hold on tight!' shouted Dr Cabbage as he turned the steering wheel furiously. Next to him, Ada gathered her cape around her shoulders and grasped the handrail as the Difference Engine began very, very slowly to turn. Dr Cabbage energetically turned the steering wheel back again, breathing heavily, as they inched around the corner.

'We weathered that one!' Dr Cabbage said delightedly as the engine slowly straightened its course. Smoke belched out of the funnel, and steam hissed inside the boiler as they chugged slowly down the country lane. 'Faster than a flying goose!' laughed Dr Cabbage, gripping the steering wheel. 'I feel the need,' he chuckled as the engine trundled on, 'the need for speed!'

An hour later they arrived at the little hamlet of Gormless. Even in the snow it would have taken half that time on foot, but Ada didn't want to hurt Charles Cabbage's feelings by saying anything. Besides, the shovel-shaped seat was very comfortable and the warmth from the boiler was lovely. Beside her, William, Heath and Robinson had curled up in the folds of her cape and fallen asleep.

As they arrived in Gormless, Ada heard music. Standing outside their cottages, the inhabitants of Gormless were listening to the village band, who were lined up beside the duck pond, which was frozen solid. The Ambridge sisters were singing a traditional song called 'Galumphing Grizelda' while the parson of Gormless St Hilda's, Dean Torville, skated around and around the pond on one leg. It all looked like a lot of fun.

DEAN TORVILLE

'Prepare yourselves!' shouted Dr Cabbage, tugging on a large brake lever with all his might. The Difference Engine came to an extremely slow halt.

'Phew!' exclaimed Dr Cabbage, pulling out a spotted handkerchief and mopping his face. 'That was a close call!'

They had come to a stop in front of a large, rather run-down building with lots of windows and doors. In front of it, a post with a sign hanging from it read:

THE GORMLESS GEORGE

COACHING INN

NO CAT SWINGING ALLOWED

Ada woke the monkeys, and just as she was climbing down from the Difference Engine a large stagecoach pulled by six horses thundered over the top of the hill. It was packed inside and out with passengers, sitting on each other's laps, grasping their luggage and hats and holding

on to handrails and hanging straps for all they were worth. Three coachmen in tall top hats sat up front, blowing long coaching horns which drowned out the sound of the Gormless Quire by the duck pond and clearly distracted Dean Torville who skidded across the ice and ploughed head first into a snow bank.

The stagecoach swerved past the sign and came to a skidding halt in front of the coaching inn. The doors of the inn flew open and the yard filled with stable boys, who began unhitching the horses while the passengers climbed down from the coach. Over the shouts of the stable hands and the chatter of the passengers Ada could hear excited barking and yapping. She walked around the back of the coach and saw it was pulling a trailer. The trailer had five compartments and sitting in each one, wagging its tail and barking, was a different dog, each with a name tag attached to its collar.

'Flossie . . . Ivanhoe . . . Emma . . . Boodles . . . Carlo,' Ada read.

'Ada!' At the sound of her name being called, Ada looked round to see Emily Cabbage making her way through the

crowded yard towards her. Dr Cabbage and the
monkeys were following.

'Emily!' Ada exclaimed and threw her arms
around her friend. 'It's so good to see you!'

'It's lovely to see you too, Ada,' said Emily,
hugging her, then stepping back. 'Did you get
my letter?'

'Just yesterday,' said Ada. 'It got mixed up among the papers on your father's desk . . .'

'So you know I made some new friends! Oh, and Ada, you must forgive me,' Emily continued, leading Ada towards one of the many doorways of the Gormless George, 'I took the liberty of inviting my new friends to Ghastly-Gorm Hall for the literary dog show – they were so excited when they heard about it. They love poets and writers!' She paused and looked worried. 'You don't mind, do you?'

'Of course not. I'd love to meet your new friends,' said Ada as brightly as she could, though she couldn't help being a little jealous. Emily hugged Ada again and then grabbed her hand and stepped inside.

Ada had never been in a coaching inn before and was fascinated to see what one looked like inside. She wasn't sure her father would approve, so she decided that she wouldn't tell him. Looking around, she saw that they were in a tiny room

filled with gentlemen sitting at small tables trying to read their newspapers without elbowing each other in the ribs or knocking over foaming drinks in tin mugs. A sign on the wall said 'Pickwick Snug – no cat swinging'.

'Excuse me . . . excuse me . . . pardon me,' said Emily politely, weaving her way across the crowded room and through another door. Ada followed and found herself in another tiny room, full of ladies trying to powder their faces without getting in each other's

way. A sign on the wall said 'Powder Room – no cat swinging'.

Beyond that room were 'The Smoking Room –

no cat swinging', which had an extremely smoky fireplace, 'The Tap Room – no cat swinging', which had very, very noisy floorboards, and 'The Waiting Room – no cat swinging', which was full of waiters. Each room was equally small and crowded. After a lot of 'Excuse me's, 'Pardon me's and 'Was that your foot? I'm so sorry's, Ada and Emily entered 'The Long Waiting Room', which was

a narrow corridor filled with passengers from the Ghastlyshire mail coach trying to find places to sit.

'Why does the Gormless George have so many rooms,' gasped Ada, who was quite red in the face from struggling through the crowds, 'and why do they all have to be so small?'

'I suppose it makes it more difficult to swing a cat,' said Emily with a shrug.*

COGWHEEL
FOOT NOTE
....
*The indoor sport of taking a cat and swinging it by the tail at a row of mouse-shaped skittles is extremely cruel and takes up a lot of space, as do goat throwing and sheep bowling, which can only be done in large barns.

They made their way over to a corner where three figures were perched on a windowsill resting their feet on their luggage, three travelling trunks with 'C.V.', 'E.V.' and 'A.V.' stencilled on the sides.

'Allow me to introduce my school friends Charlotte, Emily and Anne Vicarage,' said Emily. 'This is my best friend, Ada,' she told them.

'Very pleased to meet you,' said Ada politely.

The Vicarage sisters didn't reply. They were wearing large bonnets that cast their faces in shadow so Ada wasn't sure if they'd heard her.

'They're very shy,' said Emily, tapping

each of them on the knee in turn, so they looked up, 'and they're wearing their sonnet-bonnets. They made their own,' she explained, 'after they saw the bonnet you gave me.' Charlotte, Emily and Anne Vicarage looked back at Ada, their blue eyes glinting from the depths of their bonnets, like

CHARLOTTE

EMILY

little owls peering out from a hole in a tree.

Then, reaching up, they each unclipped a sheet of paper from the lining of their bonnets and wrote on them with a pencil, which they passed between them.

They held up the little pieces of paper.

'Delighted to make your acquaintance, Miss Goth.'

'Thank you for having us to stay. We're very excited about the literary dog show.'

'The novelists (and poet) are over there!'

Delighted to make your acquaintance, Miss Goth.

Thank you for having us to stay. We're very excited about the literary dog show.

The novelists (and poet) are over there!

Emily leaned over and whispered confidentially in Ada's ear, 'It's a little odd at first, but you soon get used to it.'

Chapter Five

As they left the Gormless George they saw that the mail coach* had left and the dog cart was now hitched to the Difference Engine, which was standing in the yard hissing and rattling as it slowly built up a head of steam. There was a crowd of strangely dressed people standing around in the yard, and Ada realized they must be the contestants of the literary dog show, the owners of the dogs.

'Well, ladies and gentlemen of letters,' said Dr Cabbage to the crowd, 'thanks to the new age of steam I'll get us back to Ghastly-Gorm Hall in no time! All aboard!'

He climbed up into the driving seat, while Ada, Emily and the Vicarage sisters settled themselves in the shovel-shaped seat beside him. Each sister had a monkey in her lap, which

COGWHEEL
FOOT NOTE
. . . .
*The next stop for the Ghastlyshire mail coach is the wool town of Baa-Baachester in the next county. Dean Torville learned to skate at the theological college there, with his good friend Anthony Wallop.

they were silently making a fuss of – tickling
tummies, stroking tails and patting heads.

'It'll be a wee bit of a squeeze, kind sir,' said
a little man with a rather large head and very
bushy white
eyebrows.
He was dressed
from head to foot
in tartan
except
for his
waistcoat,
which was
white and
covered in ink
stains. A clutch
of inky quills
stuck out from
the headband
of his tartan
top hat.

SIR WALTER SPLOTT

The Vicarage sisters wriggled with excitement and held out notes to Ada:

Sir Walter Splott!

The Highland novelist!

Writer of long leather-bound books!

'Like knights errant of old, Ivanhoe and I will venture forth on foot in quest of castle Goth . . .' Sir Walter waved his walking stick in the direction of Ghastly-Gorm Hall.

A Larnarkshire Lurcher,

finest pedigree

but a little excitable.

He opened a door in the dog cart and a large thin dog leaped out and ran around and around him, excitedly wagging its tail.

'It is a truth universally acknowledged,' said a rather stern-looking lady stepping forward to stand next to Sir Walter Splott, 'that an ambulatory perambulation is always in want of canine sagacity. We'll all walk.'

The Vicarage sisters held up signs that read:

She means Walking

is no fun

without a dog;

There was a squeal of delight from over by the duck pond where the Ambridge sisters were helping Dean Torville take off his skates. Fancyday dropped the dean's foot in her excitement, knocking him off balance and sending him head first back into a snowdrift.

'Plain Austen – the lady novelist!' she exclaimed, rushing across the yard with her sisters, Bathsheba and Tess, close behind. 'I'd know your prose anywhere!'

'It is a truth universally acknowledged that in plain speaking no other scriptress possesses my prestidigitation on the printed page,' said Plain Austen.

The Vicarage sisters held up another translation. This one read:

She's very good at complicated sentences.

'You're here for the dog show?' asked Fancyday.

'The very same.' Plain Austen opened the dog cart and released her dog. 'This is Emma, a Hampshire Blue Bloodhound of impeccable breeding and singular wit.'

'She's lovely!' said Fancyday as the wrinkly-faced dog snuffled at the hem of her dress.

A well-dressed gentleman with rather unruly hair and the biggest neckerchief Ada had ever seen stepped forward. 'William Timepiece Thackeray, at your service,' he said. At the first sight of him, the Ambridge sisters swooned and completely forgot about Plain Austen, who appeared rather disgruntled. 'High-society satirist,' he went on smoothly, taking each sister's hand in turn and kissing it. 'Show-off,' muttered Sir Walter.

PLAIN AUSTEN

74

William Timepiece Thackeray opened the dog cart and whistled.

'Boodles, Mayfair Bulldog,' he announced as a heavyset dog lumbered out. 'Blue blood, of course. I heard you ladies singing – veritable sirens of song all three of you, what-what?'

Fancyday and her sisters blushed with delight. 'If it was down to me, you'd be gracing the

WILLIAM TIMEPIECE
THACKERAY

BOODLES

London stage, not the edge of a frozen pond, what-what?'

'Well, it isn't down to you, sir,' said Dean Torville icily. He had managed to pull himself out of the snow bank and looked decidedly chilly. 'I'll expect you at quire practice,' he told the sisters before disappearing inside the Gormless George. The clatter and twang of unlikely instruments being tripped over came from the Pickwick Snug where the Gormless village band was attempting to find a place to sit.

'Country music always makes me want to dance!' exclaimed a young lady in gentlemen's

clothes, doing
a balletic jig
across the yard. She
arrived at the dog cart,
did a twirl and released an
enormous hairy dog.

'Georgie Eliot,
balletic wordsmith!' she
announced, putting a
leash on her dog's collar,
'and Flossie my Old
Middlemarch
Sheepdog.
You lead,
Flossie,
and
I'll
follow!' The old dog tugged on
the leash, and Georgie Eliot started
to sing, 'My heart is alive with the
sound of snowflakes . . .'

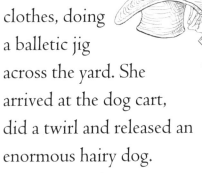

GEORGIE ELIOT

FLOSSIE

'Do you *have* to make a song and dance out of everything?' sighed Plain Austen.

'Come, Homily, join us!' exclaimed Georgie Eliot, waltzing around the yard. Leaning forward in her seat, Ada noticed an extremely small woman standing by the last compartment of the dog cart. As she watched, the woman, who was dressed in white, opened the door. A tiny black dog clambered out and stood at her feet wagging its pompom tail shyly.

'Ladies and gentleman . . .' said Georgie Eliot, doing a series of balletic leaps, 'introducing from the colonies, bedroom poet and philosopher – Homily Dickinson and her Yankee Doodle Poodle, Carlo!'

HOMILY
DICKINSON

CARLO

Homily Dickinson blushed shyly and raised the hood of her cape.

'As to what . . . I cannot . . . say but . . . afterwards . . . shall . . . if only crumpets,' she said cryptically. Carlo barked a surprisingly deep bark for such a little dog.

'Can't tempt any of you to experience the thrill of speed?' asked Dr Cabbage.

The novelists (and poet) all shook their heads. 'Very well then, see you back at the Hall – hold on tight!' cried Dr Cabbage, releasing the brake. With a hissing of steam and grinding of cogs the Difference Engine stirred into life once more and crawled slowly back along the lane towards Ghastly-Gorm Hall.

'Walkies!' The novelists (and poet) all cried as one. Sir Walter Splott, Plain Austen, William Timepiece Thackeray, Georgie Eliot and Homily Dickinson and their dogs raced past the Difference Engine and off down the lane as snow began to fall.

Ada shivered. 'Oh no!' she exclaimed. 'I've

left my cape!' It had been so hot in the coaching inn that she had slipped her cape off in the long waiting room and forgotten all about it until now.

'I'll catch you up!' she said to the others and stepped off the slowly moving Difference Engine, despite Dr Cabbage's protests that they were going much too fast and that she'd never catch up.

Ada ran back to the inn and squeezed inside. She found her cape where she'd left it on the back of a chair. Dean Torville was fast asleep on it, resting his head on the soft alpaca-wool lining. Ada did her best not to disturb him, gently easing the fabric from underneath the sleeping dean, only for Dean Torville to wake up with a start, jump out of the chair and hit his head on the low ceiling. Ada apologized profusely but the dean appeared rather dazed and didn't seem to hear her.

Slipping her cape on, Ada hurried back through the tiny rooms and out into the yard.

'Ada?' said her father's voice. 'What on earth are you doing, coming out of a coaching inn?'

Chapter Six

da felt her face begin to redden. There in the yard of the Gormless George, sitting in a magnificent sleigh which was pulled by a pair of snow-white horses, was Lord Goth. On one side of him, holding the reins, was a twinkly-eyed gentleman with a large nose. A tiny dog peeked out from the folds of his coat. On the other side of Lord Goth sat a tall woman in a cape. Her blonde hair was beautifully styled into

two magnificent plaits and her eyes were ice blue.
An even tinier dog, with a quivering nose and
enormous eyes, snuggled in her lap.

'It is the custom for the young of your country to frequent alehouses?' the blonde woman asked, then gave a tinkling laugh. 'My Viking ancestors would approve.'

THE LITTLE BARMAID

'Reminds me of the tale of the little barmaid, half girl, half herring . . .' said the gentleman with the large nose.

'Allow me to introduce you to my daughter, Ada,' said Lord Goth stiffly. Ada reddened even more. 'Her governess is on holiday,' Lord Goth told his companions, 'and it appears, in her absence, Ada is running wild . . .'

'Oh no, not wild,' protested Ada, feeling tears welling up in her eyes. She hated to disappoint her father like this. 'I came with Dr Cabbage to meet his daughter off the mail coach, Father,

84

and only popped in for a minute.'

'I'll have to have a word with the good doctor,' said Lord Goth darkly, glancing along the lane to where the Difference Engine was slowly chugging around the corner. 'But it's too cold to sit here discussing the matter. Climb up beside me, Ada, and meet the judges of the literary dog show.'

Ada stepped up into the sleigh and shook the judges' hands.

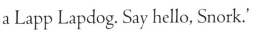

'Countess Pippi Shortstocking,' said the blonde-haired lady, 'and this is Snork, he's a Lapp Lapdog. Say hello, Snork.'

The tiny dog gave a high-pitched bark and blinked at Ada.

' "Hands" Christmas Andersen,' said the man with the large nose, raising his hands to the side of his head and waggling his extremely long fingers.

'Reindeer hands!' He laughed. 'It's my trademark, isn't it, Yorick? Yes, it is! Yes, it is! . . .' He ruffled the ears of his tiny dog.

'What sort of dog is he?' asked Ada, sitting down beside Hands Christmas Andersen. The tiny dog leaped into her lap and settled itself down.

'A Small Dane,' said Hands Christmas Andersen proudly, 'best in breed at the Elsinore Erudite Dog Show three years running, weren't you, boy? Yes, you were! Yes, you were . . .' He frowned as he ruffled the tiny dog's ears once more.

'Alas, poor Yorick was disqualified this year for burying his bone in the middle of the palace lawn. The prince went mad when he saw the mess, so we decided to

become judges instead, didn't we, boy?' said Hands Christmas Andersen. 'Yes, we did! Yes, we did!'

He took the reins and gave them a shake and the snow-white horses began to pull the sleigh. As they gathered speed, Hands Christmas Andersen began to sing. 'Tinkle bells, tinkle bells, tinkle all the way. Oh what fun it is to slide in a sturdy Volvo-Sleigh!'

Ada wanted to explain things to her father, but he was listening politely to Countess Pippi Shortstocking, who was telling him about her country estate in Lapland.

'Every year we have a flying snowman festival using giant catapults and then we go to Elsa's for frozen yogurt . . .' she was saying. 'You must come for a visit – and bring your darling daughter. Oh, Snork, do let go of Lord Goth's neckerchief!'

The sleigh was travelling fast and as they swerved around the corner Hands Christmas Andersen had to tug on the reins to avoid crashing into the slow-moving Difference Engine. Ada waved to Emily and the Vicarage sisters as they sped past. In no time at all the sleigh reached the gates to the Ghastly-Gorm estate, went through them and started down the drive.

'Whoa!' cried Hands Christmas

Andersen, tugging on the reins. Up ahead of them two carriages had crashed into each other. The horses' harnesses were all tangled up and the carriage wheels were jammed together.

As the sleigh drew up beside the carriages, two schoolboys in top hats and long knitted scarves climbed down from one carriage and a young man in expensive clothes got out of the other. He was also wearing a knitted scarf, but his was wider and longer than the others'.

'William!' exclaimed Ada, jumping down from the sleigh and running over to the youngest schoolboy. It

was William Cabbage, Emily's brother, back from boarding school in the little town of Rugby.

'Hello, Ada!' said William, turning the colours of his blue and yellow knitted scarf. William had chameleon syndrome, which meant he was very good at blending in with his surroundings.

'Wizard prang, wasn't it, Cabbage?' said the young man in expensive clothes, bounding across and knocking William out of the way. William fell over but the young man didn't seem to notice.

'You must be Cabbage's sister!' he said enthusiastically, grabbing Ada's hand and shaking it vigorously. 'Bet he's told you all about me. I'm Flushman the school chum – everybody has to be my best friend or else!' He threw his head back and roared with laughter. 'Wizard wheeze, don't you think? Decided to invite myself to Cabbage's place for the hols – they tried to leave without me but I caught up, didn't I, chums?'

'Yes,' said William bleakly. He had been helped to his feet by the other schoolboy, who was rather scruffy and seemed shy. He peered back at Ada from behind a shaggy fringe of uncombed hair. Flushman stomped off to try to disentangle the horses, laughing uproariously.

'He means well,' said William with a sigh. 'He's just a bit too enthusiastic.' He smiled. 'Now this is my good friend Bramble Vicarage . . .'

'Vicarage?' said Ada, turning to the shy-looking schoolboy. 'Are you related to the Vicarage sisters, by any chance?'

'I'm their brother,' Bramble mumbled shyly from behind his fringe. He yawned. 'Sorry, I'm rather tired. Flushman follows me everywhere. It's exhausting, though William does his best to distract him.'

Bramble looked gratefully at William, who shrugged. 'I'm good at blending in,' he said, 'and I've been keeping Flushman occupied with a game of hide-and-seek we've been playing.

'The schools of England are very keen on silly games,' he went on. 'There's the Eton Mess Wall Game, where they throw meringues at the side of a building, and the Harrow

THE ETON MESS WALL GAME

Harrumph, where everybody puts flowers in their hats and jumps in the river, and of course the Marlborough Mangle, which has no rules

THE HARROW HARRUMPH

at all . . . It keeps boys like Flushman busy so the rest of us can study.'

He looked over at Flushman, who was tugging at the reins of the carriage horses enthusiastically.

THE MARLBOROUGH MANGLE

'If only I could think of a really silly game for Rugby School . . .'*

'Allow me,' came Countess Pippi Shortstocking's voice. Ada turned to see her father and the countess standing by the tangled carriage horses. As everybody watched, Countess Pippi picked up one horse in each hand and raised them effortlessly above her head.

'How absolutely wizardly wizard!' exclaimed Flushman, as the countess held the horses in the air and Lord Goth untangled their harnesses and reins. Then she put the disentangled horses back on the ground and walked over to the carriages. She tipped first one then the other on their sides and prised their wheels apart before turning the carriages the right way up again. She dusted the snow off her hands and climbed back into the sleigh as Flushman enthusiastically whooped and applauded. 'Oh, that was nothing,' Countess Pippi

COGWHEEL
FOOT NOTE
. . . .
*Although the game of 'muddy field wrestling' is played at Rugby School, in which everybody gets as muddy as possible, it's not nearly silly enough for Flushman, who gets bored easily.

said with a smile when Lord Goth complimented her on her incredible strength. 'You should see me throw a snowman!'

'They're flying in the air,' sang Hands Christmas Andersen in an unnaturally high voice as they slid on towards Ghastly-Gorm Hall. 'They're tumbling through the midnight sky . . .'

Chapter Seven

The great-uncle clock on Ada's mantelpiece struck eight, and she opened her eyes. It was cosy and warm in her eight-poster bed, especially with the heavy curtains drawn, keeping out the chill. Ada pulled on her alpaca-wool-lined cape that she'd been careful to place at the foot of the bed the night before and climbed out from beneath the quilt. She poked her head through the gap in the curtains of her bed.

'Good morning, Miss Ada,' said Ruby, placing a tray on the more-than-occasional table beside a roaring fire. 'It's such a cold morning I thought you might like your breakfast in front of the fire.' Ruby smiled cheerfully, but Ada could see that she had dark rings beneath her eyes. Stray wisps of hair had escaped from beneath her cap and her apron strings were untied as if she'd dressed in a hurry.

'That's very thoughtful of you, Ruby,' Ada said, getting down from the eight-poster bed and joining her by the fire, 'but what's wrong? You look dreadful.'

'Oh, Ada,' Ruby exclaimed, 'what a night it's been!' Ada pulled up a chair and Ruby sat down.

'First there were strange

noises in the servants' quarters — whimpers and barks and awful growling . . .'

Ada buttered some soldiers and poured Ruby a cup of tea. 'But, Ada, I couldn't — this is *your* breakfast . . .' Ruby protested.

'Nonsense,' said Ada firmly. 'You look like you need a strong cup of tea to settle your nerves. Have a soft-boiled egg too.' She sat down opposite Ruby and patted her hand.

'I expect you heard the contestants for the literary dog show — probably just settling into their new surroundings,' Ada reassured her.

'I don't think so,' said Ruby. 'I met Arthur on the stairs this morning and he said that last night the dogs were all in the kennels Maltravers prepared for them in the Whine Cellars, right down in the vaults beneath the house. What we heard was high up at the top of the house, in the attic corridor just outside our bedrooms.' Ruby's eyes were as big as saucers. 'And then, this morning,' she continued, 'our shoes outside our doors . . .' She took a gulp of her tea.

'What about your shoes?' asked Ada.

Ruby raised her foot and pointed to a rather scratched and scuffed boot. 'Chewed!' she gasped.

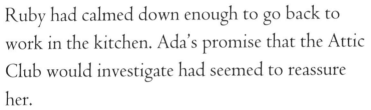

After two more cups of tea and a soft-boiled egg Ruby had calmed down enough to go back to work in the kitchen. Ada's promise that the Attic Club would investigate had seemed to reassure her.

After Ruby had left, Ada went to the wardrobe in her dressing room to get dressed. Her previous lady's maid, Marylebone, had always laid out Ada's clothes for her, but now Ada rather enjoyed doing things for herself.

She glanced out of the window. Snow lay thickly on the ground, white and sparkling in the cold winter sun.

Descending the steps in front of the Hall, Ada

saw the literary-dog-show contestants being taken by their owners for a morning walk. Or perhaps, it occurred to Ada, it was the other way round, because each of the novelists (and the poet)

had their nose buried in a book and was being carefully guided down the drive by their dog. Sir Walter Splott had an enormous leather-bound volume which he dropped and Ivanhoe the Lanarkshire Lurcher helpfully retrieved for him, his tail wagging frantically. Plain Austen was reading aloud from a novel, accompanied by elaborate hand gestures, while Emma the Hampshire Blue Bloodhound snuffled, nose to the ground, at her feet. Behind them Georgie Eliot and William Timepiece Thackeray were doing a country dance which involved linking arms and swapping the novels they were reading at regular intervals. Boodles the Mayfair Bulldog led the way while Flossie the Old Middlemarch Sheepdog herded them along from behind. Bringing up the rear, camouflaged in a white cloak and bonnet, Homily Dickinson picked her way delicately through the snow, while, black as an ink blot, Carlo the Yankee Doodle Poodle trotted by her side. As she walked, Homily recited from the slim volume of verse she held in a white-mittened hand.

'Hope is a thing with feathers,
Singing in a tree,
Alas, upon thy bough,
The cat is now,
Creeping up on thee . . .'

Her surprisingly loud voice rose up through the crisp morning air. The dogs all looked far too well behaved, thought Ada, to be guilty of chewing kitchen maids' boots. Just then there was the sound of hoofs clip-clopping over frozen snow, and down the drive came Fancyday

Ambridge in a trap pulled by a rather grumpy-looking donkey. As she passed, Fancyday waved to William Timepiece Thackeray, who interrupted his dance to give a theatrical bow in response. Fancyday tried to stop the trap, but her donkey, Maddening Claude, stubbornly continued up the drive to the front door. Red-faced, Fancyday jumped down from the trap and stomped up the steps. 'Get me far from Maddening Claude!' she stormed. 'Before I do something I'll regret!'*

Ada turned back to her wardrobe, selected the clothes she wanted to wear — a Newfoundland dress, with felt petticoat, Bergen jacket and Siberian muffler — and got dressed as quickly as she could. Ada knew that if she didn't, Fancyday would insist on picking her clothes for her and she'd spend the whole morning watching her new lady's maid going through her wardrobe, picking up and then discarding clothes that Ada would have to tidy away afterwards. Usually

COGWHEEL FOOT NOTE
....
*'Far from the Madding Claude' would later become Fancyday's first hit song in the popular comic opera 'Paint your Donkey Wagon'.

this was great fun, but today Ada had other things on her mind. She wanted to find out what had disturbed the kitchen maids' sleep and chewed their shoes. Perhaps, Ada considered, it was a ghost she didn't know about.

She poured a cup of tea and put it next to the Dalmatian divan together with a novel that Plain Austen had given to her the previous evening. She had just placed the book on a cushion when Fancyday came bursting into the dressing room, the back of her hand pressed dramatically against her forehead.

'What is a poor country girl to do,' she railed, 'when stuck with such a stubborn donkey? I was just saying to that nice friend of William Cabbage's, the one with expensive clothes, at the foot of the stairs . . .'

'Flushman?' said Ada.

'That's him,' said Fancyday, collapsing on to the divan and kicking off her shoes. 'He was hanging around in the hallway asking if I'd seen any monkeys. Well, anyway, if I had a fine horse and curricle like his, I told him, you wouldn't see me for dust! . . . What's this?'

Fancyday picked up the novel and opened it, then let out a squeal of delight. 'It's Plain Austen's latest book – *Nonsense and Nonsensibility* – in which two sisters fall in love with a couple of clowns! And she's signed it to me!' She let out another squeal. 'Oh, thank you, Ada!' Fancyday exclaimed as she accepted the cup of tea Ada handed to her. 'You are the best mistress a lady's maid could ever ask for.'

Ada left Fancyday happily reading the novel and went downstairs. There was no sign of Flushman, but Bramble Vicarage and William Cabbage stepped out from behind the large marble statue of the three pear-shaped Graces in the entrance hall.

'I think we've given Flushman the slip,' whispered William. 'Here, take this.' He handed Ada a large tea tray. 'We're meeting Emily and Bramble's sisters at the Sensible Folly. I've got an idea for a silly game,' he told her. 'I'm going to call it snow-traying.' He took Ada's arm and they crept out of the house, keeping an eye out for any sign of Flushman. Bramble, clutching his own tea tray, followed.

Outside they found Kingsley the chimney caretaker waiting for them.

'Ada,' he said, taking her to one side, 'there's something I think you should see.'

Chapter Eight

Kingsley led Ada around the front of the house to the Venetian terrace at the side of the west wing. The terrace and the lawn in front of it were covered in crisp snow, and the gnomes in the alpine gnome rockery beyond were up to their necks in a snowdrift. Kingsley stopped beside one of the Byzantine doors and pointed at the ground.

Ada looked. A set of footprints in the snow led from the doors, across the lawn and towards the hobby-horse stables behind the west wing.

'I found these this morning,' Kingsley said, leading Ada across the lawn. 'Do you notice anything odd about them?'

'Well, whoever made these footprints had forgotten their slippers.' Ada shivered. 'It must have been very cold walking barefoot in the snow.'

'Yes,' said Kingsley thoughtfully. He paused by the edge of the lawn. 'What else do you notice?'

Ada gasped. 'The footprints are changing . . .' she said, crouching in the snow and tracing the outline of one with a finger, 'into paw prints!' She straightened up. 'How very peculiar.'

'That's what I thought,' said Kingsley. 'I followed the paw prints. They lead all the way around to the broken wing and disappear inside.'

'We need to have a meeting of the Attic Club,' said Ada. 'Tonight.'

'I'll be there,' said Kingsley, 'but I'd better get to work – I've got snow to clear from my chimney stacks.' The brushes strapped to his back bristled as he clumped across the lawn, crossed the stable yard and climbed a flying buttress up towards the rooftops. Ada had just turned to go when there was the sound of wheels crunching over snow, and Lord Goth and Countess Pippi Shortstocking came around the corner. They were riding hobby horses.

'. . . but the trouble with Elsa,' Countess Pippi was saying, 'is that she'll burst into song at the drop of a snowflake. It can be quite tiresome at times . . .'

'Ah, Ada,' said Lord Goth, coming to a stop when he saw her. 'Maltravers tells me that we have an infestation

of monkeys in the library. Do you know anything about this?'

Ada blushed. 'They're working for Dr Cabbage,' she explained, 'fetching books for him.'

'Well, Maltravers caught them doing cartwheels on the furniture,' said Lord Goth sternly, with a shake of his head. 'And I'm not sure I approve of primates handling my precious books. Speaking of which, what did you think of my new book?'

Ada blushed even more. 'Oh, I haven't quite finished it yet . . .'

Her father looked disappointed and Ada felt a lump in her throat. She hated to let him down.

'It's just that I've been busy knitting jackets for the monkeys and—'

Lord Goth frowned. 'Knitting them jackets?' he said disapprovingly as his gaze fell on the tray in Ada's hands. 'Next you'll be telling me that you're taking them tea!'

Ada looked down at the ground. She didn't think her father would approve of snow-traying.

'Never mind,' said Lord Goth with a sigh. 'Miss Borgia can't return too soon in my opinion. And as for these monkeys,' he added, 'I shall have to have a word with the good doctor.' He nodded stiffly to Ada and set off with the countess across the lawn. 'Now remind me, what tree in particular are we looking for?'

'A little one,' Countess Pippi answered him as they headed towards the hobbyhorse racecourse in the distance. 'Hands Christmas Andersen is very particular about his fir trees . . .'

'There you are!' exclaimed Emily, striding across the lawn towards Ada. 'Aren't you going to come snow-traying?'

✵

Emily and Ada found the others sitting on tea trays at the top of the hill just in front of the extremely well-built copy of a Greek temple.

The Vicarage sisters each had a silver tray of their own, while William Cabbage, looking serious and concentrating hard, and Bramble Vicarage, peering shyly through his fringe, shared a large tray of inlaid teak and mahogany.

Ada and Emily placed the trays they were carrying on the ground and sat down on them.

'Girls first,' said William in a shaky voice. It seemed to Ada that he was having second thoughts about his idea.

'Come on!' Emily laughed, holding on to her
tray and launching herself down the slope.

Ada and the Vicarage sisters followed.

The tea trays took them speeding downhill in a flurry of snow, and Ada felt a delicious flutter in her tummy as her tray soared and dipped over the bumps.

At the bottom of the hill they stuck out their legs as brakes and came to a skidding, tumbling halt.

That was fun!

Let's do it again!

Race you this time!

read the Vicarage sisters' notes.

Laughing, Ada and Emily helped each other to their feet and brushed the snow from their skirts.

'This *is* fun,' said Ada wistfully. 'I wish the holidays weren't so short and we could spend more time together.'

'We could,' said Emily, linking arms with Ada

and looking out across the lake of extremely coy carp which had completely frozen over, 'if only you could come to school with me.'

'That would be lovely.'

'I think so too.'

'So do we!' The Vicarage sisters held up their notepapers.

So do we!

'I wish I could,' said Ada, 'but then my governess wouldn't have a job,' she explained, 'and Lucy Borgia has been so good to me.'

'Good morning, ladies,' said Dean Torville,

skating past on one leg. 'I've just been visiting Mrs Beat'em and saw the lake and couldn't resist . . .'

Suddenly there was a great harrumphing howl of triumph from the top of the hill and a cry of 'What a wizard wheeze!'

Looking up, Ada saw Flushman burst out from behind one of the pillars of the Sensible Folly and loom over William and Bramble Vicarage. Flushman didn't notice William, who had turned white as snow, and he leaped on to the mahogany tea tray, sending him flying. Gripping Bramble in an overenthusiastic bear hug, Flushman launched the tea tray down the slope.

'Come on, chum! We can do it!' he roared, his stripy scarf flapping behind him. Bramble's face was as white as William Cabbage's as he and Flushman hurtled downhill. As they reached the bottom of the slope the tea tray tipped up, sending Bramble and Flushman sliding across the frozen lake and crashing into the unfortunate Dean Torville.

'I say! Wizard fun!' cried Flushman, jumping to his feet and sliding across the ice tugging Bramble by his scarf behind him. 'Let's do it again!'

Ada and Emily tiptoed on to the lake to help Dean Torville to his feet while the Vicarage sisters hurried after their brother.

'I've got a better idea, Flushman,' said William Cabbage, hurrying down the slope and gently releasing Bramble's scarf from Flushman's enthusiastic grip. 'Why don't we play hide-and-seek, just the two of us?'

'Yes,' said Bramble gratefully, 'just the two of you.'

'What are we going to do about Flushman?' Emily Cabbage asked. 'Poor Dean Torville sprained his ankle and broke one of his skates. And the Vicarage sisters are worried about Bramble. They keep exchanging notes about him but won't let me see.'

It was late, and the Attic Club was holding a special meeting.

Emily handed the wooden spoon to William, who had turned the colour of the hessian coal sack he was sitting on.

Arthur Halford, Kingsley Travers, Ruby

Kipling and Ada sat on the bean-filled coal sacks around the fruit-crate table and waited for their turn to speak. Moonlight flooded through the round attic windows, bathing the floorboards in a silvery light.

'I played hide-and-seek with him all afternoon,' said William, 'just to give Bramble a break. Then he wanted to look at Father's inventions in the Chinese drawing room and was very disappointed to find a "Do not disturb" sign on the door.'

William frowned. 'I feel a little sorry for him. You see, his father ignores him — keeps packing him off to Rugby School even though he is far older than the rest of us.'* He handed the spoon to a worried-looking Ruby.

'Well, that's as maybe. But what the kitchen maids and I want to know is who or what has been chewing our boots.' She shuddered. 'Mrs Beat'em's noticed and accused us of playing football in the

COGWHEEL
FOOT NOTE
. . . .

*Josiah Flushman the water-closet tycoon was extremely busy manufacturing toilets and sadly lost interest in his son soon after he was potty-trained.

126

corridor after bedtime – she's on the warpath.' She
passed the spoon to Arthur Halford.

'I don't want to worry anyone, but last night
I looked out of my window in the stables and
saw something creeping across the stable yard,'
he said. 'Something hunched and hairy and
wearing a stripy scarf that looked like your friend
Flushman's.'

Ada accepted the wooden spoon from him.
'Kingsley showed me the footprints this morning.'
She looked from face to face in the moonlight. 'I
think the Attic Club needs to keep a close eye on
Flushman,' she
said quietly.

Chapter Nine

'The theme of our dog show is Christmas!' announced Hands Christmas Andersen, raising his hands to his head and spreading his long fingers. 'Reindeer hands!' He chuckled. That morning the library had been cleared of wing-back chairs by the hobby-horse grooms, closely supervised by Maltravers. Now, as everyone gathered in the grey afternoon light, Ada saw that a large wooden barrel filled with earth had been placed at the centre of the enormous Persian carpet. Planted in it was a small but beautifully proportioned fir tree from the grounds of Ghastly-Gorm Hall.

'Baubles!' cried Hands Christmas Andersen. 'Where are my Christmas baubles?'

'They're here, in your flying trunk,' said Countess Pippi Shortstocking. She nodded with a swish of pigtails to Arthur Halford and Kingsley the chimney caretaker, who each grabbed a handle of the large trunk and carried it over to the tree.

'Why is it called a flying trunk?' asked Ada, who was standing on the edge of the carpet with Emily and the Vicarage sisters.

'Because it came all the way from Turkey in a hot-air balloon,' explained Hands Christmas Andersen. 'Fascinating story — I must tell it to you sometime. Now, let's see what we have here . . .'

He opened the trunk and reached inside. When he withdrew his enormous hands, they

were full of sparkling glass globes decorated with swirls, stars and snowflake designs.

Skipping around the little fir tree he began to festoon it with baubles, his fingers a blur of movement.

'In my country it is too cold to go outside to the tree!' he declared. 'So we bring the tree inside!'

Reaching back into the trunk, he pulled out coils of glittering ribbons and wound them around the tiny tree. Then he took armfuls of candles that he crammed on to the small branches, then

tiny parcels, little striped candy canes and small plump cherubs coated in gold leaf.

'And we celebrate the festive spirit by decorating this, the symbol of the forest. One day everyone will have a beautiful little fir tree at Christmas, decorated just so!'*

He stepped back and examined his handiwork. The little fir tree had completely disappeared beneath the jumble of glittery, sparkly, shimmering decorations. Reaching into the flying trunk one last time, Hands Christmas Andersen took out a small doll dressed in blue and white with an oversized head on a spring. He carefully placed the doll at the very top of the little fir tree and waited until its head had stopped wobbling.

'Elsa the show queen!' he said, stepping back. The literary-dog-show contestants, who should have been watching but had been distracted by the shelves of books, looked up from the leather-bound volumes they had selected and politely

COGWHEEL
FOOT NOTE
....

*Unlike the Christmas tree, some festive traditions, such as elk decorating and sugar-plum bobbing, have never caught on.

applauded. At their feet their dogs' tails thumped on the Persian carpet as they wagged. Over by the door, holding Belle and Sebastian's leash tightly, Maltravers eyed the decorations on the little fir tree with interest.

'The Ghastly-Gorm literary dog show will take place here in the great library tomorrow night, on Christmas Eve,' announced Lord Goth, who was standing by the mantelpiece watching proceedings. He looked rather serious and Ada thought he was avoiding catching her eye.

'Countess Pippi Shortstocking and Hands Christmas Andersen will be the judges,' Lord Goth told the contestants.

'There will be three rounds,' Countess Pippi said, stroking her Lapp Lapdog, Snork. 'The first round will be fetching, the second will be musical walkies . . .'

'And the third round,' said Hands Christmas Andersen with a flourish of fingers, 'will be jumping!' Elsa's large head wobbled

on top of the little fir tree, and from Hands
Christmas Andersen's top pocket Yorick's little
doggy head appeared.

The Vicarage sisters gave a shudder of
excitement and gathered around him.

Hands Christmas
Andersen settled himself
on his
flying
trunk and
the sisters
took turns
petting Yorick
the Small Dane.

'I don't suppose you've heard the tale,' Hands Christmas Andersen said, spreading his fingers in an expansive gesture, 'of a wild young man of the moors and his encounter with an intense young governess while out looking for a house to rent?' The Vicarage sisters shook their heads.

'Once upon a time . . .' Hands Christmas Andersen began, and went on to tell a long, involving story that held the Vicarage sisters spellbound.

Meanwhile Maltravers had been taking a closer look at the tree, and Ada was sure she spotted him slipping some baubles into his pocket.

She was just about to go over and challenge him when she saw the door at the far end of the library open and one of the monkeys enter the room. Ada glanced over to see if her father had noticed, but he was deep in conversation with Countess Pippi Shortstocking, who was cradling Snork in her arms. Ada nudged Emily, and they both watched as the monkey, wearing the suit

Ada had knitted him, sidled over to one of the windows and vanished behind the curtains. A few moments later, the monkey emerged, eating a banana. It opened the door and slipped out. The next moment the door opened and William Cabbage stumbled in, helping a dishevelled Bramble Vicarage.

'I shouldn't have suggested playing corridor football,' said Bramble as he was helped to sit down on a library ladder. 'Flushman was a little overenthusiastic and squashed the football, then pushed me downstairs.' Beside him William looked around nervously.

'If it's all the same to you, I think I'll take supper in my room,' Bramble mumbled. 'I don't feel quite myself.'

'You were meant to be keeping an eye on Flushman, William,' said Emily crossly.

William turned the colour of the leather-bound volumes behind him.

'That's easier said than done,' he said.

Just then Dean Torville limped into the library and waved a greeting to Lord Goth. 'Thank you for my invitation to dinner, Lord Goth,' he said:

'Whoaaa!'

The dean came crashing to the floor as his foot
slid on a discarded banana skin.

Lord Goth, Ada, Kingsley and
Arthur all rushed over to help him
back to his feet.

Lord Goth picked up the banana skin and
looked at Ada. 'I'm going to have to speak to the
good doctor,' he said ominously.

Chapter Ten

'My lord, ladies, novelists and poet,' Maltravers announced in a dry, wheezing voice, 'dinner is served.' They were sitting around the enormous table in the steam-engine dining room of Ghastly-Gorm Hall. A model railway track led out of a Corinthian-columned serving hatch in the far wall and along a viaduct to the dining-room table. The track went around the table in a big loop, then back through the hatch and down to the kitchens. A small steam engine ran along the track, pulling carriages containing dishes from Mrs Beat'em's kitchen. The diners could serve themselves as the steam engine chugged slowly past.

Charles Cabbage, who was sitting at the far end of the table with William, Emily and Ada, took a whistle out of his waistcoat and blew it twice. Down in the kitchens there was a distant clatter as the kitchen maids loaded the carriages, followed by the sound of chugging which grew rapidly closer. The dog-show judges, novelists and poet all leaned forward expectantly, their eyes on the Corinthian serving hatch.

Suddenly there was a billow of steam through which a small steam engine emerged. It had a tall funnel, fast-moving pistons and a shovel-shaped scoop at the front, similar to the seat of the Difference Engine. Charles Cabbage smiled delightedly and, from beneath the table, three little heads in red hats popped up.

'A new invention of mine,' said Charles Cabbage, 'which I think your father will appreciate. I call it the cake-catcher. Not yet . . .' he said to William, Heath and Robinson. 'I'll let you know when it's time.' At the other end of the table, Ada saw her father looking over at Dr Cabbage. He wasn't smiling.

The steam engine chugged down the viaduct and slowly around the table, pulling carriages laden with Mrs Beat'em's first course of Constantinople artichokes, coddled whelks in regret-me-not sauce and a large tureen of Ghastlyshire gruel.

Around the table there was the clink of cutlery as the guests helped themselves.

Flushman elbowed William Cabbage in the ribs as he scooped a large portion of coddled whelks into his own bowl.

'Where are the Vicarage sisters?' Ada asked Emily.

'They're having supper with their brother in

his room,' said Emily. She sounded concerned. 'They're very worried about him.' She glanced over at Flushman, who was tossing whelks to the monkeys and laughing uproariously. 'We must try to help.'

The steam engine disappeared through the hatch and a few moments later the clatter in the kitchen increased.

'Tell me, Doctor,' said Lord Goth, leaning back in his chair, 'what progress have you made with your calculating machine?'

Dr Cabbage swallowed a mouthful of Ghastlyshire gruel.

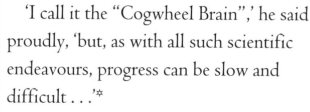

'I call it the "Cogwheel Brain",' he said proudly, 'but, as with all such scientific endeavours, progress can be slow and difficult . . .'*

'Surely, Doctor, performing primates can only serve to distract you from your work,' said Lord Goth, fixing the monkeys with a stern look, 'not to mention hazarding the safety of my dinner guests.'

Next to him Dean Torville, his arm in a sling, struggled with his Constantinople artichoke.

'Ah, yes, the banana skin.' Dr Cabbage's face reddened. 'Rather unfortunate . . .'

COGWHEEL FOOT NOTE
. . . .
*Charles Cabbage's Cogwheel Brain is indeed one of the miracles of the modern age and unrivalled in its calculating and computing capabilities, even if I do say so myself.

148

'As was taking my daughter to a coaching inn,' said Lord Goth icily.

'But, Father, I explained . . .' began Ada, only for Lord Goth to silence her with a wave of his hand.

'I'm not angry,' he said. 'Just very disappointed.'

He turned to Countess Pippi Shortstocking and Hands Christmas Andersen, and smiled. 'Tell me, how are you enjoying our simple country fare?' he asked, as the steam engine chugged back into the dining room, travelling faster, smoke billowing from its funnel and carriages hurtling behind it. A partridge pie, a pigeon pie and a plover pie, each bigger than the one before, were followed

by potted rabbit, jugged hare and jellied goose on increasingly large platters.

William Timepiece Thackeray gallantly served Homily Dickinson and Georgie Eliot as the steam engine rattled past, but not without splattering Plain Austen with a poorly aimed spoonful of jellied goose.

'It is a truth universally acknowledged that a dining companion with food stains is in want of a napkin,' she said sternly.

Flushman was enjoying himself enormously and grabbed most of the partridge pie as, gathering speed, the steam engine chugged past.

'Wizard grub!' he exclaimed enthusiastically, showering William in crumbs.

The steam engine disappeared back through the serving hatch.

'My dear Lord Goth,' said Dr Cabbage, calling for hush by tapping the side of his glass with a spoon, 'and esteemed guests, allow me to demonstrate my latest invention . . .' He turned to the monkeys. 'Now!' he said.

William, Heath and Robinson jumped up and proceeded to run along the table placing small cakes on the tracks in front of each guest.

The sound of chugging grew louder and the
steam engine came careering through the serving
hatch at considerable speed, towing a row of
jugs containing raspberry, caramel and white-
chocolate sauces. The engine raced down the

viaduct and on to the table.
It scooped up the first
cake on the track with its
cake-catcher, sending it
flying up in
the air and
down into
a sauce jug.
Reaching out
a spoon, Homily
Dickinson plucked
the raspberry-coated
cake out of the jug
and into her pudding
bowl. The cake-
catcher scooped up a
second then a third cake, and the guests helped
themselves as the cakes landed in the sauces.
Lord Goth looked impressed. The steam
engine sped around the table and Flushman
grabbed three cakes in one go and tossed them

to the monkeys with a laugh.

'Delicious,' said Ada, tasting a white-chocolate-covered cake, 'and so clever.'

'Yes . . .' said Dr Cabbage hesitantly as the engine left the dining room at increasing speed, 'but I think it might need a little adjustment . . .'

Shouts and cries of dismay sounded in the distance, and there was the crash of dishes falling on flagstones. Mrs Beat'em's booming voice sailed up from the kitchens – 'Quick! The cheese course! Now!'

A few moments later the steam engine shot through the serving hatch at full pelt, swerving on to the viaduct and swaying perilously as it sped towards the table. This time Gorgonzola globes, mini-truckles of Gormless Blue and Cheddar Gorgeous and wedges of Wessex Whiff lay jumbled across the cheeseboards in the carriages, while cheese

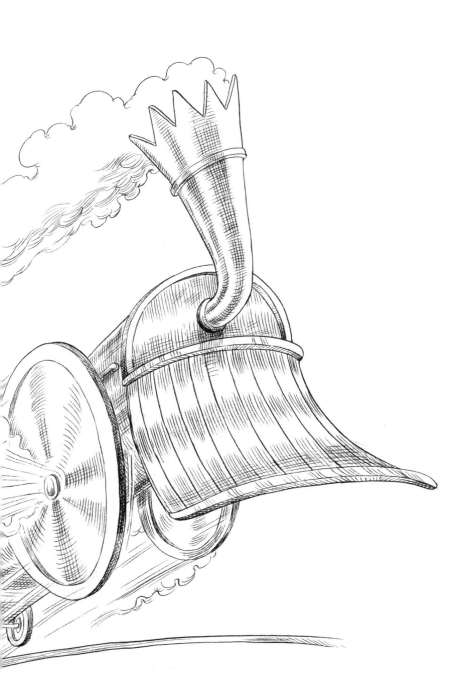

straws in haystacks wobbled along behind.

'Shield yourselves!' cried Sir Walter Splott as the engine careered around the first bend and several carriages overturned, sending truckles and cheesy globes flying through the air.

'It is a truth universally . . . unckh!' exclaimed Plain Austen, as a truckle of Gormless Blue jammed itself in her open mouth. 'Oh, the humanity!' exclaimed Homily Dickinson, ducking beneath the table as Gorgonzola globes rained down. Lord Goth gallantly shielded Countess Pippi Shortstocking with a raised arm as cheese straws filled the air.

Going too fast to take the next corner, the steam engine shot off the table and came crashing to the floor, overturning in a cloud of steam. The cheese carriages followed, with what was left of their contents melting in the heat of the engine.

'It's a fondue fiasco!' declared William Timepiece Thackeray.

Flushman dipped a finger in the melted cheese and licked it.

'Wizard cheese crash!' He laughed.

Lord Goth brushed cheese straws from his immaculately styled hair and got up from the table with as much dignity as he could muster.

'I don't understand it,' Dr Cabbage was muttering, parting strands of Gorgonzola and examining the crashed steam engine. 'I distinctly remember setting it to "dinner service",' he said, tapping the speed dial, 'but someone has turned it to "fast food" . . .'

'Dr Cabbage,' said Lord Goth. His voice was calm and quiet, but Ada could tell from the look in his eyes that he was angry. He removed a cheese straw from behind his ear and dropped it on the floor.

'This is the last straw.'

Chapter Eleven

'What was that?' asked Emily, slipping down under the covers. It was the sound of a low moaning whimper rising to a mournful call, soft and distant, as if somewhere in the grounds of Ghastly-Gorm Hall a small wolf was howling at the moon.

'It's probably just a ghost,' said Ada. 'Possibly the second Lady Goth's Prince Rupert Spaniel, who bit Oliver Cromwell, or maybe Peejay, the bald Irish Wolfhound who haunts the Whine Cellars. It's far too cold to go and investigate now though.' She pulled the quilt up beneath her chin. 'Where were we?'

Ada and Emily were having a sleepover in the eight-poster bed and Ada was enjoying hearing Emily's tales of school life. Neither of them had managed to eat very much at dinner, but while the kitchen maids had cleared up the mess in the steam-engine dining room, Ada and Emily had wrapped slices of pie and chocolate-covered cake in napkins and taken them up to bed.

'West Wuthering is smaller than Gormless and doesn't even have a coaching inn,' Emily said, 'but it is very pretty, and we go for long walks on the moors most mornings.'

'It sounds lovely,' said Ada longingly. 'Would you like the last piece of cake?'

'You have it, Ada,' said Emily, snuggling down further under the covers. 'Then when we get back, Charlotte, Emily and Anne write down stories they've thought of on our walks. They're very good writers, you know.' Emily smiled sleepily. 'There's one called *The Glass Town Girls*, about three girls from Africa who visit England,

and one called *The Girls from Gondal*, about three Japanese princesses, and my favourite, *Look Back in Angria*, about an imaginary kingdom where three short-tempered girls are

always having adventures.'

'I'd love to read them,' said Ada, wrapping the last of the cake in a napkin and putting it on her bedside table. She blew out the candle and pulled the curtains shut around the bed.

'If you came to school, you could,' said Emily wistfully. 'They write them in tiny books in very neat writing . . .' Her voice trailed away. In the darkness, Ada couldn't see her face.

'Your father was very cross with my father,'
Emily continued. There was a tremble in her voice
as if she was trying very hard not to cry. 'My father
says that if he doesn't make faster progress with
his Cogwheel Brain, Lord Goth will ask him to
leave here.'

Ada reached out and gave Emily's hand a
squeeze. 'Try to get some sleep,' she said. 'Things
will seem better in the morning; they always
do.'

Not that Ada really believed this. Lord Goth
had looked very stern and his mood hadn't been
improved by Dean Torville burning a finger on
some molten Cheddar Gorgeous on his way out of
the dining room. Ada closed her eyes. She would
have a proper talk with her father after the literary
dog show. If she couldn't talk him round, she
might never see Emily again.

In the distance a plaintive howl rose up in the
frosty night air.

✻

Ruby the outer-pantry maid woke them early the next day.

'Mrs Beat'em's very cross with your dad for ruining her dinner last night,' she told Emily as she put down the breakfast tray. 'Says she's going to complain to his lordship, and that's not all.'

'It isn't?' said Ada, climbing out of bed and putting on her cloak.

'No,' said Ruby, her eyes wide. 'Someone's made a terrible mess of the inner pantry and stolen a leg of ham. Mrs Beat'em suspects one of the dogs and she's absolutely furious. She's had words with Maltravers, but he said all the dogs were locked in their kennels in the Whine Cellars last night and rattled his bunch of keys at her.' She shuddered. 'Then Mrs Beat'em started throwing plates . . .'

'Sit down, Ruby,' said Ada, 'and have a nice cup of tea.'

After breakfast, Ada and Emily got dressed,

then put on large Scotch berets and knitted Hibernian mufflers and went outside. Fancyday had just arrived with her sisters and the rest of the Gormless Quire to rehearse the music for the dog show, and Ada waved to her as they unloaded

their unlikely instruments from a hay cart and carried them into the house. 'Mr Thackeray says I'd be perfect for a part in the musical adaptation of his satirical novel of country life,' Fancyday trilled, much

to her sisters' irritation. 'It's called *Vanity Fete* –
perhaps you've heard of it. Anyway, see you at
the show!'

Ada and Emily found the Vicarage sisters in
front of the west wing, making a snowman with
William, while Bramble Vicarage looked on
shyly, his hands thrust deep in the pockets of his
coat.

They had piled the snow into an impressive
mound for the snowman's body, so Ada and Emily
helped the sisters to roll a big ball of snow. Then
William and Ada picked it up and put it on the
snowman's shoulders. Emily took off her mittens
and began to sculpt the snowman's head while the
others watched.

'She's very talented,' wrote Charlotte Vicarage
on her notepaper.

'We love her drawing,' wrote Emily Vicarage in
neat capital letters.

'We'd like her to illustrate our novels one day,'
wrote Anne Vicarage.

'I'm sure she'd like that,' said Ada. 'Emily was telling me about your stories last night. I'd love to read them one day.'

She turned to Bramble, who was looking at her from behind his unruly fringe. 'What about you, Bramble?' she asked. 'Do you write stories or draw pictures?'

'No,' he said shyly, 'but I like to act out parts in my sisters' stories when I go on long walks on my own.' He looked down at his feet. 'What I'd really like to be is an actor but, like my sisters, I have the family curse of shyness.'

'I'm so sorry,' said Ada sympathetically, 'but perhaps you'll grow out of it.'

All four Vicarage children stared down at their feet miserably.

'What do you think?' asked Emily Cabbage, turning to the others.

'Excellent!' said her brother, 'but how about this for a finishing touch?' He reached down and picked up the ham bone lying in the snow at his feet. It was white and glistening, with teeth-marks along its length. Reaching up, William pushed it into place on the snowman's face.

'Now who does that remind you of?' he asked, smiling.

'Hands Christmas Andersen!' said Ada. She turned to Emily. 'You don't suppose that's the leg of ham stolen from Mrs Beat'em's kitchen, do you?'

'Or what's left of it,' said Emily darkly.

Chapter Twelve

A full moon had risen in the sky, bathing Ghastly-Gorm Hall in a silvery light. The snow glistened and twinkled on the ground and the frosty air was filled with the sound of carriage wheels crunching on frozen gravel as guests began to arrive for the Ghastly-Gorm literary dog show. On the steps of the Hall, dressed in a magnificently embroidered Albanian overcoat and sheepskin fez, Lord Goth stood ready to greet everyone. Ada and Emily, wrapped up warmly in their Hibernian mufflers and Scotch berets, watched from behind one of the tall classical columns of the portico.

First to arrive was Lord Goth's oldest friend, Lady George, Duchess of Devon, without her three plump Dalmatians. 'I left my girls at home,

Goth,' she told Ada's father as he greeted her. 'With such literary hounds on show I didn't want Lottie, Dottie and Spottie to feel inferior – they're *so* sensitive.'

She was followed by what Lord Goth called 'the Grate and the Should' (but only in private). They were people from other large houses in Ghastlyshire and the neighbouring county of Baa-Barchestershire, who grated on one's nerves and thought they should always be invited to things. Lord Goth smiled politely as the Twistle-Ton-Ploughly-Hews, the Dossington-Gruffs and the Mutter-Chuffs of Mithering Grange arrived all at the same time and pushed and jostled each other as they squeezed through the front door. They were followed by the Woolfs of Willoughby Chase, Sir Orlando and his daughter Virginia, who had the habit of looking down her nose at people.

'I do hope that tiresome village band won't play too loudly,' she said haughtily. 'I swear the

playing of rustic instruments makes me want
to become a lighthouse keeper. The
sound of the waves is awfully
soothing, I find.'

Finally a battered chariot
drawn by three horses
pulled up and two
gentlemen climbed
out and stretched
their legs. One was
thin and smartly
dressed, and the
other was portly
and scruffy.

'Well done, Troilus,
Pyramus and Thisbe,'
said the portly
gentleman, patting the
horses. He gave them
each a carrot, then
turned to Lord Goth.

THE WOOLFS OF WILLOUGHBY CHASE

'Sir Christopher Riddle-of-the-Sphinx R.A.,* canine caricaturist,' he said, shaking Lord Goth's hand. 'And this is Mr Christopher Priestley of Cambridge, the distinguished novelist. *Hair and Hounds* sent us to cover your event, Lord Goth.'

'Gentlemen of the press,' said Lord Goth with an icy smile. Ada knew her

COGWHEEL FOOT NOTE
....

*Sir Christopher is a well-known illustrator of literary dog shows and, along with William Morris-Minor the kennel wallpaper designer, is a founder of the Arts and Crufts movement.

MR CHRISTOPHER PRIESTLEY

SIR CHRISTOPHER RIDDLE-OF-THE-SPHINX R A

178

father wasn't keen on journalists, whom he blamed for spreading stories about his habit of taking potshots at his garden ornaments, giving him the reputation of being 'mad, bad and dangerous to gnomes'.

'Do try to keep out of the way,' he said through gritted teeth as he showed them inside.

Ada and Emily followed.

The great library was crowded. The gold chairs that the hobby-horse grooms had laid out were all occupied, leaving standing room only. The Vicarage sisters had tried to save seats but had been too shy to stop Sir Orlando and Virginia from taking them, so Ada and Emily found a place at the back, by a bookcase beside a curtained window. The leather-bound volumes rippled, and William Cabbage stepped away from the bookcase.

'Put your shirt on and stop showing off!' Emily told him. At the front, sitting on a gold seat, Charles Cabbage was applauding enthusiastically

as Countess Pippi
Shortstocking and Hands
Christmas Andersen took
their seats next to the
ornately decorated fir tree.
Lord Goth sat down next
to Charles Cabbage and
gave him a stern look.

'You can get a better
view from up here,' came
a whisper, and, looking
up, Ada saw Bramble
Vicarage halfway up a
library ladder. Ada,
Emily and William,
who'd put his shirt back
on, climbed up to join
him.

'I'm feeling a little odd,' whispered Bramble
to Ada. 'I think all these people are making my
shyness worse.'

'Don't worry,' Ada tried to reassure him. 'You're among friends.'

'Talking of which,' said William, looking around the library anxiously, 'has anyone seen Flushman?'

'I spoke to Kingsley and Arthur when they were fetching the chairs,' whispered Bramble. 'They said they saw him sneaking into the library with a squashed football and a bunch of bananas, but when they came back there was no sign of him.'

'Let the literary dog show begin!' said Lord Goth in a loud but elegant voice.

The contestants and their dogs, each with a capital letter attached to its collar, were standing by the bookcases that lined the far wall, facing the audience. As they waited, the novelists, poet and indoor gamekeeper brushed their dogs' coats, fluffed up their fringes and combed their tails.

'Round one,' said Countess Pippi Shortstocking. 'Fetching.'

Hands Christmas Andersen got up from his chair and walked to the far side of the library. He held up his hands dramatically. He was clutching six leather-bound volumes, one written by each of the contestants, which he proceeded to shuffle like a deck of cards before spreading them out on the floor. At the opposite side of the library, Countess Pippi invited Sir Walter Splott to sit in a wing-back chair which she had turned, effortlessly, to face the wall. Ivanhoe sat at his master's feet.

The audience shifted expectantly in their chairs.

'Fetch!' commanded Sir Walter Splott. Ivanhoe sprang to his feet and trotted over to the books, which he sniffed one by one. The Lanarkshire Lurcher gave a little sneeze, then picked up an extremely long novel about a poorly dressed Highlander and returned to the wing-back chair, only to have a sneezing fit as Sir Walter reached for the book. *Drab Roy* clattered to the

floor. The audience groaned and Countess Pippi
Shortstocking and Hands Christmas Andersen
exchanged a look. Sir Walter Splott dabbed at
the cover of the book and then licked his finger.
'Pepper!' he muttered.

Next Plain Austen crossed the floor and sat in
the wing-back chair, Emma at her feet.

'Fetch!' she commanded. Emma loped over
to the books and snuffled over each one in turn

before selecting a novel about an ambitious carriage driver called *Northanger Cabbie*, only for the book to slip out of her mouth and slide across the floor. Emma tried to pick it up, but again it slid from her mouth. The audience groaned.

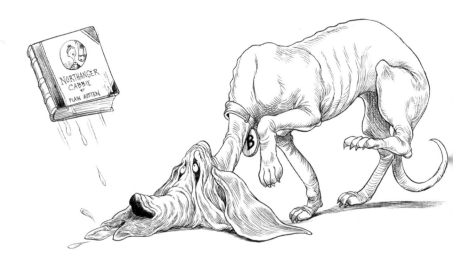

'The cover of this book has been greased with butter!' Plain Austen protested, leaping up and attempting to grasp her novel, which slipped out of her hands, shot across the room and hit Dean Torville on the nose.

'Poor loser,' muttered Maltravers with a smirk.

William Timepeace Thackeray didn't fare much better. 'Fetch!' he ordered Boodles, who raced over to the copy of *Vanity Fete* and picked it up. The audience was about to applaud when Boodles began to dribble uncontrollably and dropped the book.

'Mutton fat,' said William Timepeace Thackeray darkly, sniffing the book's cover.

'Fetch!' commanded Georgie Eliot, who had danced over and sat down in the chair. Flossie gambolled over and picked up a novel about dentists in Lancashire. As she carried *The Floss in the Mill* over to her owner, Flossie began to foam at the mouth and spat out the book. The crowd groaned. Georgie Eliot picked the foaming book

up with a thumb and forefinger and inspected it.
'Soap!' she exclaimed.

Homily Dickinson walked over to the wing-
back chair and sat down nervously. Carlo the
Yankee Doodle Poodle looked up at her with
large, anxious eyes.

'Fetch!' Homily Dickinson said in a small,
trembling voice. Carlo pitter-pattered over to the

books and gingerly picked up a slim volume of verse. He carried it over to the chair, trembling as he did so.

Maltravers gave a sharp, explosive sneeze, and Carlo, startled, dropped *Of What I Speak Thou Knowest Not* on the floor. The crowd groaned.

'I couldn't help it.' Maltravers shrugged and gave a dusty smile.

He walked over to the chair flanked by Belle and Sebastian, their pompom tails wagging excitedly. Maltravers sat down and crossed his legs casually.

'Fetch!' he wheezed. Belle and Sebastian raced over to the other side of the library, picked up Lord Goth's latest volume of poetry, *The Pilgrimage of Harolde the Kid*, each taking a corner,

and carried it back to Maltravers. The indoor
gamekeeper picked the book up and held it aloft
triumphantly.

The audience applauded.

'Round two,' announced Countess Pippi
Shortstocking. 'Musical walkies.'

Beside her, Hands Christmas Andersen held
his arms up to his head, fingers spread wide like
antlers. At this sign, the Gormless Quire, who had

been waiting patiently by the fireplace, struck up a lively country jig.

The six contestants with their dogs on leads began to walk in a circle, in time to the music, around a row of five wing-back chairs that Arthur Halford and the hobby-horse grooms had placed in front of the audience.

Hands Christmas Andersen wiggled his fingers and the music stopped. Quick as a flash, the contestants flung themselves as elegantly as they could into the chairs. Homily Dickinson and Carlo both gave surprisingly loud yelps of frustration at finding all the chairs were taken. Hands Christmas Andersen's fingers froze and the band resumed playing. A chair was removed.

'I left my heart in Budleigh Salterton,' sang the Ambridge sisters in harmony. William Timepeace Thackeray and Boodles swooned at the sound. The music stopped. 'Blast!' said the satirist when he found he was the only one left standing.

The music began again, another chair was taken away by Arthur Halford, and Ada waved to him from her vantage point on the library ladder.

The music stopped. Plain Austen was left standing. 'It is a truth universally acknowledged

that . . .' she began, only for the band to start playing again. Plain Austen stomped over to Virginia Woolf of Willoughby Chase, who was covering her ears, and sat down huffily.

The music stopped just as Sir Walter Splott was doing a Highland jig.

'Our joust is done!' he told his Lanarkshire Lurcher sadly.

Only Georgie Eliot and Maltravers were left as the music began again.

'I was only twenty-four hours from Salisbury,' sang the Ambridge sisters.

Georgie Eliot pranced balletically around the single remaining chair, Flossie galumphing after her on the end of a tight leash. Maltravers strode around the chair flanked by Belle and Sebastian. He reached into his pocket and stealthily dropped a clutch of Christmas baubles, sending them rolling across the floor. The music stopped and Georgie Eliot leaped high in the air towards the empty chair.

'Eek!' she cried as Flossie tugged her in the opposite direction, chasing the baubles. Georgie Eliot landed inelegantly on the seat of her breeches as Maltravers sat down in the last wing-back chair. Belle and Sebastian leaped up into his lap and the audience applauded.

Ada, who didn't like cheating, shook her head. She wasn't the only one though. Lord Goth obviously shared his daughter's feelings, because he got up and walked over to his indoor gamekeeper, speaking sharply to him in a low voice. He wagged his finger and Maltravers hunched low in the wing-back chair, scowling. When he had finished, Lord Goth straightened up and said in a loud, but elegant voice, 'Round three will be the decider, and everyone –' he gave Maltravers and the poodles his sternest look – 'will abide by the rules!'

Out of the corner of her eye Ada saw a flash of movement, and turning her head she saw that the three monkeys had slipped into the library and were tiptoeing past the bookshelves towards her. Each of them was carrying a bundle of papers from Charles Cabbage's desk in the Chinese drawing room, covered in calculations scrawled in green ink. As Ada watched, a hand emerged from a crack in the curtains.

It was holding a
banana.

'Round three!' said
Hands Christmas
Andersen clapping
his hands together.
'Jumping!'

Chapter Thirteen

The literary-dog-show contestants and their dogs lined up against the wall of the library, a look of intense concentration on every face.

Countess Pippi Shortstocking raised her arm. 'At my signal, each dog must jump over the little fir tree,' she told them, 'making the show queen's head wobble as little as possible.'

She dropped her arm and Sir Walter Splott released Ivanhoe. The Lanarkshire Lurcher sprinted across the floor and leaped high over the little fir tree, the tip of his long tail just grazing the top of Elsa's oversized head.

The show queen gently nodded and Countess Pippi Shortstocking and Hands Christmas Andersen shook their heads.

Plain Austen urged Emma the Hampshire Blue

Bloodhound forward, but she was so used to snuffling along with her nose to the ground that she just bumped into the wooden barrel and set the baubles bouncing.

Elsa's oversized head nodded furiously. When it had stopped, Boodles the Mayfair Bulldog bounded forward and leaped with all his might, only to hit the little fir tree on his way down.

Hands Christmas Andersen caught the falling show-queen doll in an outstretched hand and put her back on top of the tree. Ada crept back down the library ladder, followed by William, Emily and Bramble. Her eyes were fixed on the monkeys, who had slipped, almost unnoticed, to the curtained window, their backs to the wall. The audience oohed and aahed as Georgie Eliot's Old Middlemarch Sheepdog, Flossie, sprang over the little fir tree with surprising ease, her long shaggy coat just brushing the show queen's crown. Carlo the Yankee Doodle Poodle did his best, but misjudged his take-off and ended up clinging to a bauble while above him Elsa's head wobbled in a blur of movement.

Ada tiptoed towards the window as, one after the other, the monkeys slipped behind the curtains.

With barks of excitement Belle and Sebastian bounded towards the fir tree from two different directions, crossing in the air high over Elsa the show queen's head, which showed not a flicker of movement, the wide-eyed expression frozen on her oversized face.

'Yes!' cried Maltravers as the poodles landed and bounded back to his side.

Ada gripped the curtains and pulled them aside. Flushman, carrying a squashed football stuffed with Charles Cabbage's papers, was climbing out of the window. The three monkeys looked guiltily back at her, bananas in hand.

'Stop, thief!' shouted Ada, and all heads turned

in her direction. With a shout of 'Wizard wheeze!' Flushman ran towards his curricle, which was waiting on the frozen drive.

Countess Pippi Shortstocking sprang into action, charging across to the window and vaulting through it.

Flushman reached the curricle, leaped into the seat and urged his horse on.

'He's getting away!' cried William Cabbage, following the countess out of the window.

'Not so fast!' said Countess Pippi, striding over to the snowman in front of the west wing.

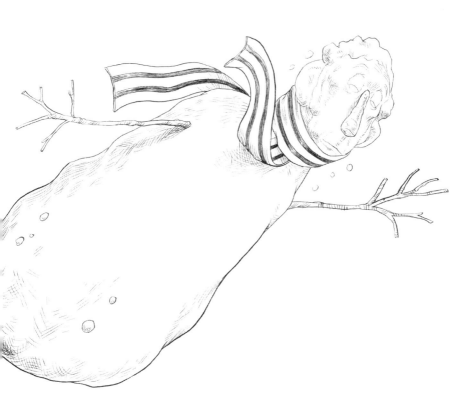

Seizing it by the arms, she lifted the snowman above her head and launched it high into the night sky.

As Ada and the others watched, the snowman flew through the air and came down, smashing into Flushman and knocking him off the curricle.

Picking himself up, Flushman made a run for it, only for the countess to to tackle him around the legs. As he hit the ground, the squashed football was knocked from under his arm and sailed up into the air. William sprinted forward and caught it cleanly.

'This has given me an idea for a game,' he said thoughtfully.

'Bramble!' came a shriek from behind Ada. 'What's happening to you?'

'Make it stop!'

Ada turned. The audience had shrunk back to the corners of the great library and the Vicarage sisters had dropped their notepapers and were standing on their chairs shrieking in high-pitched voices.

'Bramble!'

'Bramble!'

'Bramble!'

Bramble Vicarage was standing in the moonlight, which was streaming through the open window. His fringe was growing heavier, his nose was getting longer and his teeth sharper. He stared down at his hands, which were changing into claws, and behind him a long, wolfish tail was beginning to wag.

'I don't feel quite myself . . .' he growled, then threw back his head and howled at the moon.

'Oh, Bramble!' wailed the Vicarage sisters. 'You look a fright!'

'But I feel . . . wonderful!' Bramble roared and

with another howl he leaped past Ada and out through the open window.

'Stop him, please,' the Vicarage sisters pleaded, 'before he hurts himself!'

'You've found your voices!' said Emily Cabbage, wide-eyed.

Ada climbed out of the window, followed by the sisters, Emily and William.

'Everybody stay calm,' said Lord Goth in a loud but reassuring voice as he stepped through the window. 'We have experts in canine ways present, do we not?'

'We certainly do,' said Hands Christmas Andersen, stroking the head of Yorick, who'd popped up out of his pocket to see what all the commotion was.

Halfway down the drive, Bramble was alternately howling at the moon and singing snatches of 'I left my heart in Budleigh Salterton' in a surprisingly tuneful voice.

The village band and the Ambridge sisters

climbed out of the window and began to play along.

'He seems happy,' said Charlotte Vicarage, wiping her eyes.

'The boy's a little wild,' said William Timepeace Thackeray, 'but he has talent . . .'

Bramble leaped high in the air, did a somersault and landed on his furry feet. He turned to see Flushman standing next to Countess Pippi Shortstocking in the snow.

'Flushman!' Bramble roared, his fur bristling as he clawed at the ground. 'I'm going to tear you limb from limb!'

'Save me!' squealed Flushman, leaping into the countess's arms.

Just then a dark shape passed over the moon. Looking up, Ada saw a large bat-like shape swoop down. There was a swish, a glint of metal and the rattle of a chain as the figure landed. It bent over Bramble for a moment, then straightened up. There, standing in the moonlight, with Bramble straining at a silver leash, was Ada's governess, Lucy Borgia.

'Looks like I arrived just in the nick of time!' she said with a smile.

'I've seen this sort of thing before,' said Lucy Borgia, settling into her wing-back chair beside the fire. The guests had all left and the hobby-horse grooms had tidied up in the library. Maltravers had taken the dogs to the kennels in the Whine Cellars and was now with the other dog-show contestants in Mrs Beat'em's kitchen, showing off the purple sash the judges had presented him with.

Ada had never seen him so happy, and he had even apologized to the others for his 'little tricks' in the first two rounds. Hands Christmas Andersen and Countess Pippi Shortstocking had done a great job of calming Bramble down, and his sisters were now taking turns to comb his fur in front of the fire as they listened to Ada's governess.

'It is sometimes a bite from a werewolf, but often it can just be a stray bit of drool, accidentally touched while out on a ramble . . .'*

'Bramble does love to walk on the moors,' said Charlotte Vicarage, smoothing his fringe as he lay sleepily on the carpet.

'We all have wildness within us,' said Lucy Borgia, smiling at the sisters, 'and it is often strongest in the shyest ones. Bramble now needs to learn to control his inner wolf and use it to his advantage. Hands and Pippi here can help him with that.'

COGWHEEL FOOT NOTE
. . . .
*While out for a walk on the moors, Bramble brushed past some werewolf drool on a gorse bush left by a hairy typographer called the Hound of the Baskervilles.

'We'll do our best, of course,' said Hands Christmas Andersen, and Countess Pippi Shortstocking nodded. 'I had a boyfriend who was a timber wolf at weekends. Very well-behaved the rest of the time,' she told Lucy.

'They often are,' said Lucy Borgia. 'The Beast of Bodmin was in fact a well-mannered librarian, and the Horror of Hackney ran a respectable bookshop near Victoria Park. Unfortunately werewolves are often misunderstood and things can end very badly.' She smiled at Ada, who was sitting

THE TRONDHEIM TIMBER WOLF

THE BEAST OF BODMIN

THE HORROR OF HACKNEY

at her father's feet. 'Luckily for all concerned, we caught Bramble in time.'

'Will he remember anything in the morning?' Ada asked.

'Not at first. This might have been happening for a while without his knowledge.' Ada thought of the chewed shoes and the howling in the night. 'But the more he accepts his condition, the more he'll remember, until, once every full moon, he'll be able to fully express himself, safely.'

Lucy Borgia knelt down and ruffled Ada's hair. 'Now, there's something I need to tell you,' she began. 'Your father and I have discussed it and—'

'My dear Lord Goth,' said Charles Cabbage, striding into the library, William and Emily following behind him. Emily's eyes were glistening. 'I can't apologize enough for my monkeys' appalling behaviour. The love of bananas is no excuse. Flushman has confessed everything. It seems he wanted to get his father's attention and believed he could impress him by passing off my inventions as his own . . .' Dr Cabbage smiled. 'He shows promise though – just needs to curb his enthusiasm a little. I shall offer him a job in my new workshop in London—'

'You're leaving Ghastly-Gorm Hall?' said Ada, leaping to her feet. 'But you can't . . .' She turned to Emily.

'I have imposed on your father's hospitality for

long enough, Miss Goth,' said Dr Cabbage, 'and with my own premises I will make real progress on my Cogwheel Brain.'

'But when will I see you?' Ada asked Emily. She had a lump in her throat, but was determined not to cry.

'All the time.' Emily smiled, tears in her eyes.

'That's what I wanted to tell you,' said Lucy Borgia softly. 'I too am leaving Ghastly-Gorm Hall. It is hard, but knowing you are happy will make it easier. You see, I have accepted a post in His Regent's Secret Service.' She smiled. 'I'll be Lord Sydney Whimsy's right-hand agent, 008.'

'And I have decided,' said Lord Goth, getting to his feet and holding out his arms to Ada, 'to send you to school with Emily.'

'Oh, Father!' Ada exclaimed, and rushed into his arms.

Epilogue

'What an eventful holiday it has been,' said Ada, 'but I can't wait to start school.'

They had planned to buy tickets on the Ghastlyshire mail coach, but Lord Goth wouldn't hear of it. Instead he had provided his finest coach and horses to take Ada, Emily and the Vicarage sisters to West Wuthering. Charlotte, Emily and Anne had been very taken with Lord Goth and had started to put dark, handsome, brooding characters into their stories. After being so shy for so long, the fright Bramble had given them had allowed the sisters to find their voices and now they talked and told stories all the time. William Cabbage had returned to Rugby School where, according to his latest letter, he had introduced some new games, including the addition of a squashed football into the school game of 'Muddy Field Wrestling'. This was a great success and was keeping overenthusiastic pupils fully occupied so those like William could get on with their studies. As for Flushman, having left school he was proving to be a very hard worker, and Charles Cabbage was very pleased with him. At his workshop in King's Cross, the Cogwheel Brain was almost finished. What was more, Dr Cabbage had more than fifty monkeys usefully employed and the organ grinders of London were absolutely furious about it. Bramble Vicarage, meanwhile, had gone to Denmark to study with Hands Christmas Andersen and Countess Pippi Shortstocking and was making great progress.

Emily Cabbage reached out and took Ada's hand. 'I can't wait either,' she said.